STEINWEG

Hendrik Roelofsen

Steinweg

Kupoteya njia ndiyo kujua njia

To get lost is to learn the way

Swahili proverb

One

Sarah was pissing angry. Jeremy and she had spent a swell romantic evening together in a fine restaurant. Good food, great wine, plenty of laughter. And as an obvious extension they had made passionate love in Sarah's place. On the kitchen table, on her couch and in her bed. Now he was gone. 'Sorry, I can't stay', had been his simple announcement, before he grabbed his coat and headed for the door. Not even a thank-you-and-goodbye kiss or 'I'll call you'. Plain nothing.

It was two o'clock in the morning and in six hours she would have to be in her shop, but she was too upset to go to sleep. Sarah picked up a beer can from the table, which was still half-full, and hurled it at the wall. 'There, asshole, that's for you!' But of course, Jeremy was no longer there. It was not in her habit, Sarah's, to fall into a tantrum; in fact, Sarah thought of herself as a civilized and sophisticated lady, but tonight she had had it! 'Men!' she shouted, 'I hate you!'

Jeremy had come into her life, or rather crossed her path, only ten days ago. After a series of disastrous relationships Sarah had opted for a break. A period of solitude. "Better be happy alone, than unhappy together" had been her motto and for over a year she had stuck to it. Yes, there had been plenty of opportunities for dating and more; after all she was considered attractive and full of mischievous energy. Her work brought her into quite a few interesting social circles and numerous young and not so young men had asked her for a date. She had refused: 'Sorry, there is nothing wrong with you and I'm not a lesbian. But right now, dating is not my game. Good luck elsewhere!'

Until last week that is, when Jeremy literally crossed her path. Every Sunday morning, if she were in town and weather permitting - although Sarah was not the one to submit to weather circumstances - she would be out there in the park, jogging. Like on that spring Sunday morning ten days ago. She recalled the circumstances of her accidental encounter with Jeremy, there and then, but right now she would rather forget.

'Asshole!' she said once more, but with a bit less conviction than a few minutes ago. All of a sudden she felt tired, drained of the life-giving juices that had flowed so abundantly earlier in the evening. She sat down on her couch, watching the drops of beer leaving traces on her freshly-painted wall – not unlike Jeremy's semen having left a trail on her belly and legs. 'Disgusting!' she uttered and fell asleep.

Two

'Stupid bitch', Jeremy said. No, he did not say it, but he *thought* it. He had gone for his routine cycling exercise in the park. That was his thing. He didn't like workouts – boring – nor did he like ball games, but cycling gave him a kick. What he liked about it was, among other things, the rapidly changing scenery around him when peddling away. There was so much more to see when cycling then when walking or jogging. He would often spend his vacations on his bike, going up mountain passes and down hidden valleys, taking it all in with passion: the adrenaline of the exercise and of the beauty of nature.

During the weekends it was only exercise: he would take the bike lane in the park not far from his apartment and cycle his rounds. Routine was three times around the 10 km-long circular track. He would not be the only one on Sunday mornings: many others had a similar passion, moving along with similar speed and a solid white line painted on the asphalt separated those going in opposite directions.

"Bikes only" it said on signboards placed at frequent intervals. For obvious reasons: bikers and walkers don't mix. They have different motives for being out there, and their moves differ accordingly. Jeremy was going at a steady 30 km/h pace when suddenly a moving "something" appeared on his retina. It was a jogging person, coming out of the bush on his right, obviously ignorant of having taken a collision course with cyclists. Jeremy pulled his brakes with full force and yelled. Too late: he rammed into the jogger, skidded and Jeremy, his bike and the other person ended up in one messy heap.

Jeremy's initial anger dissipated quickly: there was a situation to be addressed. He got up – no bones broken – and reached out to the other person, a woman, to help her on her feet. 'Are you hurt?' 'I don't know, I'm sorry.' He looked at her and his nasty thoughts of a few seconds ago were instantly replaced by another reflection: what a beautiful woman!

Jeremy righted his bike and inspected his body. A few scratches her and there, but nothing serious. However, the woman was clearly in pain and bleeding. Jeremy made her sit down next to the track and started to inspect her injuries. 'It probably looks worse than it is, let it bleed a bit and once you get home, clean it up with some antiseptic. Nothing broken, I hope?' The woman didn't respond to Jeremy's remarks and was possibly in a light state of shock. He looked at her and again thought: what a beauty!

Jeremy was not what you call a ladies' man. Yes, being 45 years old, he had had his share of women in his life, had even been married once, but his current interests were elsewhere. Yet, he recognized a beautiful woman when he saw one and this crumpled being belonged into that category.

'Listen, if you want I can help you clean up. I live close by and have all the first-aid stuff you might need. What's your name?' 'Sarah Appleton. Thank you!' 'Jeremy, pleased to meet you', he said with some irony. He helped her up, put his arm around her waist, picked up his bike by the handlebars and gently started the procession to his home. He lived in a penthouse overlooking the park and it took them only ten minutes to get there. He chained his bike next to the front door and guided Sarah to the elevator.

Jeremy had not lived for very long in this building. In fact, he had been a bit of a wanderer throughout his life, moving from one place to another, one country to another. Settling down somewhere for long he had found stifling. Not that the grass was greener at the other side of the fence. It just was *there* and might provide fresh challenges. And by accepting those challenges, he might emotionally and intellectually grow-up.

In the process he had amassed considerable means, financially that is. Recently he had decided to give travelling a break and to settle in the city, not his city of origin, but the city of his business and to see what happened. Through an agent he had found this penthouse and, although it was horrendously expensive, had bought it on the spot. That was six months ago. Since, he had decorated it, using the many artifacts he had collected during his travels and complementing those with other unusual items he picked up at auctions and flea markets in the city. The end result he found rather pleasing: an interior reflecting the richness of human creativity and an exterior, the view, the even richer magic of Mother Nature. Altogether he was pleased with what he had found for himself and, at least for the moment, had no intention to leave.

'Please, sit down here', Jeremy said after Sarah and he had entered his apartment, 'while I'll get my stuff. But first have some water.' He filled a glass and handed it to her.

Sarah had to some degree regained her presence of mind. Not entirely, but sufficiently to be conscious of the situation. She had left her flat this morning for a simple jogging exercise to be followed by a lazy afternoon. At her place. Here she was, with her body in an unknown state of shambles, in the apartment of a total stranger. Not quite the scenario she had in mind. That, she knew, was one of her character traits: wanting to control things and being rather unhappy when she couldn't. That trait was debit (or credit – she had not decided) for her current status of "bachelorette", for her "better being happy alone than unhappy together" credo. So, there she was, out of control.

Of late there had been occurrences of questions presenting themselves spontaneously: was she making the right choices, was she making choices at all, was there such a thing as "right or wrong"? But other than registering the thoughts, Sarah had not moved on them. No, that is not true; she had put them in a drawer for future reflection.

She was pointedly aware that hormones were a formidable force in human's lives and short of being explained, they shouldn't be ignored. She was now approaching thirty-eight and were motherhood not to be given a last chance? If so, would that entail a dual-parent arrangement? And who be the other half? If not, would she forever regret? Valuable and important questions, that had bubbled up in her mind of late, but this was not the moment to ponder; there was an emergency here to be dealt with. And was she in control? It didn't look like it.

Jeremy showed up with his first-aid kit. During his travels he had learned that being equipped with basic medicaments, bandages and dressings could be of life-saving significance and even in the "civilized" world he had maintained the habit of keeping his "toolbox" in good order.

'Now, let's give this mess a proper look-over', he said, almost as if talking to a child. He had a pair of scissors in his hand. 'Do you mind if I cut off the legs of your jogging pants?' Sarah didn't care: she'd much rather spent money on a new pair of jogging pants then, if that were the alternative, let this stranger have a gander at her knickers. 'Please, do what you think is best', she replied meekly.

Jeremy went to work, cleaning the abrasions, taking out pieces of gravel, cleaning again, dabbing iodine on the various damaged body parts ('Aii, that hurts', Sarah exclaimed), sprinkling antiseptic powder generously, cutting pieces of compresses and taping those gently on the affected areas. He went about it as a skilled practitioner and Sarah couldn't help feeling a sense of comfort coming over her: surrendering, in a situation of helplessness, to a guy who seemed to know what he was doing, was not a bad sensation.

Having attended to her cuts and scratches Jeremy took position in front of her, like a painter checking out his latest strokes on a canvas. 'I think we have that under control', he announced, almost pontifically, Sarah thought, 'but that's the outside. The inside I cannot see and I suggest that you visit a doctor as soon as possible. Meanwhile, does it hurt anywhere? Move your legs, your feet, your arms, your head. Any discomfort?' Sarah did as told. 'No, a bit sore here and there, but no particular pain anywhere. But I will ask for a check-up with my doctor, tomorrow, as you suggested.'

Jeremy went to his fridge. 'Some more water, something else?' he asked while he grabbed a beer. 'No, thanks', Sarah replied, 'I think I should be heading home.' 'As you wish,' he reacted, took a first gulp of his beer – he always enjoyed that after his biking exercise – and pulled up a chair in front of Sarah. 'Chill a bit. I propose that I get out of my cycling gear, take a shower and walk you home. Where do you live?'

Sarah began to realize that, while both Jeremy and she had been in an accident, one had taken care of the other in a disproportional way. It could have been Jeremy with bruises and broken bones and she would have to administer first-aid, or something. Fortunately, he wasn't badly hurt, but she hadn't even inquired about his condition. *He* had taken charge and the situation seemed to be under *his* control. Was that bad? Was that against her principles? And then there was another question, which almost made her panic: did she owe Jeremy something? If so, shouldn't she quickly get into damage-control mode?

'I live only two blocks away, on the Boulevard des Fripiers. I'll manage, don't you worry', was her defence. 'No', Jeremy protested, 'give me five minutes and I'll see you home.' Sarah did not care. She wanted this situation to be over and if

Jeremy was to be in charge, so be it. After Jeremy got freshened-up they left his apartment and headed for the Boulevard des Fripiers.

Jeremy knew this neighbourhood and admired its 18th century architecture. He had even checked out a few apartments, but finally had fallen for "a room-with-a-view" and bought his own on the Avenue des Princes. 'Jeremy, I live right here at number 136. Once more, I'm terribly sorry for what happened today and for having screwed up your Sunday morning. Many thanks for taking care of me. I'm OK now and will find my way. Enjoy the rest of your Sunday.'

'As you wish', Jeremy responded, 'but I wouldn't mind having your telephone number, just in case there would be a need for some insurance follow-up.' Sarah did not quite grasp what this "insurance follow-up" could entail, but she gave Jeremy her number anyway. 'Take good care of yourself', he said and took the road back to his place.

Sarah's apartment might not have a view over the park, like Jeremy's, but it was otherwise a superb dwelling. High beamed ceilings, marble floors and arched separations between the various living spaces. Sarah did not own it – she resisted having "possessions" – but had fallen in love with it when looking for a place to live after her last relationship had painfully fallen apart. She could easily imagine the grandeur of past times and the lifestyles of the rich merchants who had created their palaces, before the buildings had been divided in separate units. Not that she cared about "the past"; it was just that old-fashioned beauty and charm seemed to suit her. The relationships she had been in almost always meant shacking-up with her partner of the moment and having been rather disappointed in the added-value of sharing, she had decided not only to give up on men, but also to find a place that felt like hers and hers alone. A year ago she had found this apartment, and, with the consent of the owner, had done some renovation work, decorated it in style and now felt very happy. This was her place. Her life.

Three

Sarah sank into her couch and let out a big sigh. It had been quite a morning, but it was not the *accident* that had drawn energy out of her. It was the *incident*, the happening itself, that puzzled her. Why had that occurred? She knew her jogging routine and, with a stretch of imagination, all the pebbles on her path. Why had she veered off the track and ventured into unchartered territory today? Yes, she recognized that she had been in thoughts, but what had those been, before she was rudely awakened by the physical encounter with that cyclist? Now, trying to replay the course of events, she hardly could remember his face; it was the question of *why*, that preoccupied her with overwhelming intensity. *Why* was she distracted? Was there a force of life at play, a sign that read: time for change? Had she arrived at the crossroads of something that needed to be acknowledged? Sarah sighed once more. 'I don't know and I'm tired. I'd like to think about it some other time', she said to herself.

But she didn't manage to clear her head during the remainder of the day. She felt like a marionette, with an unknown player pulling the strings in a random rhythm. It was not totally unpleasant, just rather unsettling. She tried to read the Sunday paper, but, lacking concentration, put it aside. She switched on the TV, zapped through a few channels and switched it off again. She made herself something to eat, but decided that she did not feel hungry and put her concoction in the fridge.

The phone rang. She picked up the receiver: 'Hello?' 'Sarah? Hi, it's me, Jeremy. I just wanted to know how you're doing.' In the confusion of today Sarah had almost forgotten a major actor in the events: Jeremy. 'Oh, it's you. Fine, I'm fine, I guess.' 'Any complications?' Jeremy wanted to know. 'I don't think so, but to tell you the truth I haven't really looked. Not even taken a shower', Sarah replied. 'I'm a bit disoriented, but nothing serious. No concussion, I believe. Maybe a light state of shock. Thanks for calling, anyway.'

'Listen', Jeremy suggested, 'I had lunch with a good friend of mine, a doctor. I told him about our accident. He lives in my apartment building and would be happy to see you today.' 'No, I'm fine. Thank you very much. I will try to see my own doctor first thing tomorrow morning', Sarah reacted.
'I hope that will work out and that there will be no unpleasant surprises. I'll call you in the evening. No, I have a better idea: let's have dinner together tomorrow night.' 'Yes, that would be fine. Where?' 'You like Italian? At "Chez Enzo?" Seven thirty?' 'See you tomorrow and goodnight.'

Sarah put the receiver down and stood still frozen. What had she just done? She had accepted an invitation for dinner from a total stranger. For over a year she had avoided men and refused dates, out of principle, and now, without a nanosecond of reflection, she had said "yes". Was she going mad? This was too much to handle in one day: her accident, her confusion and the break with one of her principles.

Four

Sarah's doctor agreed to see her right after she gave him a call Monday morning. He examined her, took some X-rays and found all in order. 'Who put on those dressings? Very expertly done, but have them changed every two days', he counselled. Damn it, Sarah thought, would she have to go back to Jeremy and to undergo the humiliating experience of him looking after her again? Having agreed on a date was already bad enough – she had thought of cancelling when she woke up this morning, but she did not have his telephone number. Yes, she knew where he lived, or at least thought that she would be able to find his apartment, but she did not want to take that route and most likely he would be at work (whatever that might be). 'OK, many thanks, I will take care of that', she had said, before leaving the doctor's office and heading for her shop.

It would be a busy day today. She had many appointments, both with visiting clients and calls to make in the city. Sarah thought of herself as a responsible individual and that included being punctual. Immediately after she had woken up she called her assistant Terry at home and told that she might be late arriving at the shop. 'Maybe half an hour or so,' she had said. 'Can you please look at my schedule and see to it that we don't screw things up?'

That was all that Terry needed as instruction, being this efficient organizer. Terry had been working with Sarah for the last five years and had become Sarah's alter ego. Sarah's business was difficult to describe; she considered herself an "interior decorator" but in fact she did much more and her clients could be very demanding. A resourceful PA like Terry embodied the difference between success and failure. And, partly, thanks to Terry, Sarah's business had become very successful.

There was also something else: from childhood Sarah had developed a very independent lifestyle, which was also reflected in her choice of sports. She enjoyed the big outdoors, mountaineering, sailing, skiing, but on her own. She would often be away for weeks on end, without contact with home base. And then it was Terry who kept things going. Sarah could not do without her.

Her schedule had been perfectly rearranged when Sarah arrived at her shop and she went straight for it. But not with her usual cool and professional zest. The sense of confusion she had experienced yesterday was still there. Again: it was not the confusion that bothered her; it was the question of *why* she felt that way. It was not Jeremy; she was sure of that – for as much as one can be sure of anything. It was not the date with him tonight, but the fact that she had accepted his invitation was certainly part of the confusion. Why did she feel this way, so totally anchorless, so terribly footloose?

During the whole day her soul-searching persisted, at the detriment of her work. She could not blow the thought-storms away. It drained her emotionally and once more she considered cancelling her date, calling in sick, so to speak. But she didn't, and even admitted to a certain excitement about her dinner with Jeremy. After all, it had been a long time since she had been in the exclusive company of a man, socially that is, and who knows: she might enjoy it.

Sarah arrived at "Chez Enzo", true to style, at 7:30 sharp. Jeremy was already there and got up from his table to greet her. She looked him over: shit, he was handsome! A wild mane of black hair, dark eyes to match, and his sporty frame accentuated by a white silk shirt and tailored black pants. But it were not his looks that struck Sarah: it was the energy that this man radiated. Positive energy, flowing from an inner source that said: "harmony"!

Before accepting his extended hand, Sarah noticed a strange sensation: the confusion she had felt yesterday and today had made place for a sense of "calm". But that in turn, and paradoxically, confused her again: what was going on with her? Jeremy took her hand: 'Thanks for coming, Sarah, and nice to see you again. This time not laying on a bicycle track or being in my apartment for treatment of your injuries. I hope you have recovered.'

Jeremy pulled out a chair for her to sit on and gently eased her towards the table. And a gentleman, she thought. Sarah was an emancipated woman; tonight, she felt, she wouldn't mind being treated like a princess.

'Do you care for a drink, before we order?' Jeremy suggested. Sarah doesn't drink alcohol, or hardly, but that did not seem to matter now. 'I would love to; a glass of Chardonnay please.' When the waiter came, Jeremy passed the order, including a Chivas – no ice, please – for himself. They toasted, he looked into her eyes and Sarah, like when she had first entered the room, felt his energy flowing into her. This is a man who is very, very comfortable with himself, she thought, and a man who can make feel other people, like me, very comfortable as well.

Jeremy asked about her doctor's visit and whether he had diagnosed any further damages to her body. Sarah gave him a summary report and Jeremy didn't ask any further questions.

'Tell me something about yourself', he encouraged her instead. Sarah is, what she considered, a very private person, keeping her thoughts and other personal details to herself. Tonight she had no difficulties with opening-up. On the contrary, she considered it comforting, sharing some of her life's stories with this man.

'Well, you know where I live now', she started, 'but I've been around. My father – he passed away – was a diplomat and every three or four years our family moved to another country. In the process I've seen many places and was exposed to many cultures. I've probably become a bit of a stranger to myself as a result.' Why was she saying that? Sarah thought. Was that the truth, and if so, why would she share that with Jeremy? Jeremy didn't say anything, but kept his dark eyes fixed on her in a warm and trusting way.

Sarah continued and her stories moved like rapids in a stream, accelerating and halting at unpredictable intervals. She recounted events and emotions she had never put into words before, or even into thoughts. She told Jeremy how much she had loved her father, how she had detested her mother – who also had passed away – and how much she regretted having lost all contact with her twin brother. Hearing herself talking like that, Sarah felt if it was someone else's story, not hers, and stopped. 'I'm sorry. I'm talking too much. I don't know why I'm telling you all this. I must be boring you. What about you?'

'You're not boring me at all', Jeremy instantly reacted. 'In fact your stories move me and I would love to hear more. Yes,

I will happily tell you a few things about myself, but before doing so I have a question for you, and that is this.' His eyes rested glued on hers. 'I sense something very special about you. What is it? What is your secret?'

Sarah did not respond and her eyes wandered away. And so did her mind. What was happening? She felt at the same time floating and firmly grounded. Floating, because of the lightness of her body, grounded because of the security Jeremy appeared to provide. 'Can I have another glass of wine, please?' was all she could come up with.

'Of course', Jeremy replied and signalled the waiter: 'The same please and can we have a look at the menu?' The drinks and menus were delivered; they toasted again and began to explore the extensive choices on offer. Sarah put the menu away: 'I let you choose for me.' Another thing she had never done before. As a matter of course, she always insisted on making her own decisions.

'OK, you asked about my "secret". I'm not aware that I have one. But I'm aware that I've received invaluable gifts in my life. In spite of what I just said – having become a stranger to myself - , my exposure in my youth to many different cultures has been a very enriching experience. If there is a secret in my life, something or someone that has shaped me, that or who welded it together into who I am today, it is my father. He was an extraordinary man. Full of humility, at the same time a man of great strengths. His values were of the highest standards and, I believe, he succeeded in transferring some of those onto me.'

She stopped there, reflecting on what she had just said. Yes, her words correctly captured her feelings, but why had she not spoken those words before? Not to her father, before he passed away, not to anybody else? Why now to Jeremy? Jeremy did not react, other than saying: 'I'll order for you. Some oysters for starters and afterwards a grilled sole "al limone". I'll have the same.'

'Let me ask you another question: what is the meaning of love for you?' 'Wow, that's a heavy one', Sarah replied, blushing slightly. 'I assume you talk about "romantic" love. Well, I've been rather disappointed in that department. I don't know whether it has been me, the other one, or just circumstances. But it has been painful, to the point that I have decided to give it a break and... to give up hope.'

Sarah hesitated. She did not like to bare her soul, not to close it either, certainly not for Jeremy. And she definitely didn't want to be a cry-baby, soliciting help from friends, leave alone from the man in front of her. Yet, she had told him things that she had not shared with anybody else. Why?

And then Sarah started to cry; not a few tears leaking out of the corners of her eyes, no, wholesome sobbing. Jeremy did not say anything, did not do anything, not even offering her a Kleenex. After what looked like an eternity to Sarah, she uttered some words: 'Oh Jeremy, I'm so sorry. I don't know what's happening to me. Maybe I should go home.'

'No, please don't leave and don't feel sorry. What's happening *has* to happen for reasons you and I don't know. Certainly, there is a reason for your sadness and I'm quite comfortable with not knowing what that reason might be. I gratefully accept this moment, your presence and surrender to not knowing its meaning. Can you try to do the same?'

Sarah was silent and in thoughts: here she was making a total fool of herself, in front of a stranger (although less of a stranger as time passed) and this stranger considered her behaviour "normal"? The waiter arrived with the oysters. Sarah asked to be excused: 'Jeremy, let me go to the powder room and repair the damage.' Sarah doesn't wear make-up, but at least she wished to dab her face with cold water to recompose herself. 'Take your time', Jeremy suggested gently, 'the oysters are already cold.'

The dinner was very pleasant; Jeremy asked no "further questions", Sarah avoided venturing into tear-provoking territory. There was no prying into each other's private life.

There was a sense of unchallenged comfort. 'Jeremy, will you let me pay for dinner?' Sarah asked after coffee was served. 'After all, you saved my life.' 'I reckon that your life is worth more than the price of a dinner. No! But if there is a next time, I'll accept with pleasure.'

They left the restaurant. 'I'll walk you home', Jeremy said without expecting a reply. He took her arm and they didn't speak a word until they arrived at Sarah's front door. 'Thank you for a lovely dinner, Jeremy. And once more, I'm sorry for the scene I made. Good night.'

She hesitated and before Jeremy could say anything, she continued: 'If you have the time and if I don't impose myself too much, could you please help me and change my bandages tomorrow night?' 'With pleasure', Jeremy replied with his deep voice. Only now Sarah realized how much his voice was part of that comfortable presence Jeremy represented. 'I expect to be home around seven. And in case you don't remember: I live on the Avenue des Princes, number 312. Take care and sleep well!' He kissed her on her cheek and disappeared into the night.

It was not late, around nine o'clock. Sarah normally didn't go to bed before eleven. She liked reading and happily spent the end of her days lying on her couch with a good book. She intended to do so tonight. It was not to happen; yes, she laid on her couch, book in hands, but she did not read. She burst out in tears. It was a super burst; if possible, double the intensity of the previous one, at "Chez Enzo". Now being on her own, she let it go. There were no thoughts attached; her crying seemed simply to be a spring-time cleaning of her system: body and soul, but no thoughts. Sarah just let go. After half an hour (an hour?) she felt dried up. And then thoughts started to enter. Not in any particular order of time or significance (how would she know?), but they were there and Sarah surrendered to being a spectator.

Five

There was this decision of hers, taken a year ago, to see no men, there was this accident yesterday morning, caused by unexplained circumstances, there was the confusion afterwards, there was the acceptance of a dinner invitation against her principles, there were a series of anomalies in her ways of doing things in general, exchanging established and comfortable character traits for rather unchartered behaviour. Sarah took those observations in as effects, but now was very curious as to the causes. Would her past deliver any clues?

Her life, in spite of frequent moves, had been rather a straight line. Yes, there had been crossroads, but very few cul-de-sacs. As a child she had an interest in the arts, both visual arts and music. Her parents had encouraged her to take piano lessons and she had quickly picked up the basics. In the process, Sarah had recognized that she had a good ear and a knack for improvising. But she had also realized that she would never make it to a professional rank. The same applied to painting: she doodled a bit and played with colours, but it did not reach – and would never, she knew – Picasso levels, or even those of minor gods.

When time came to make a university choice, she let herself be inspired by her father and his profession. She chose political science. Sarah thoroughly enjoyed student life and got a kick out of organizing campus clubs and events, but the subject of her studies she had found boring. Seeing her father at work was fascinating, reading theory about his work was not.

After two years she opted out and went to art school. Intuitively she felt that was where she belonged, but she did not stay. She did not see herself becoming a professional artist and certainly not one who could make a living out of selling her works, were they to find a market at all. Yet, her stint at the art school – also two years – taught her, or rather confirmed, something else: whenever the students had a "project", an outing, an event, an interaction with the school management, it was Sarah who took the lead or was called upon. Sarah had organizing skills and using those gave her pleasure. Lots of it! She briefly thought of enrolling in a business school, but decided against it. She had enough of schools and rather developed her own ideas.

A plan started to take form in her head: she was an independent woman; professionally she wanted to be independent too. She had her hobbies, which she wanted to pursue whenever she felt like it, being it sports or anything else. Yet, she had a few things to learn, and more importantly: to build up a network of contacts.

That was another lesson she had learned from her father. He had been in many global trouble spots and often been instrumental in solving thorny issues. In a private moment with Sarah he once told her that the key to success – at least in his profession – was patience and access to key players. Patience, Sarah had not much. She felt comfortable with that admission. Access to key players she did not have either and she was not comfortable with *that*.

Building up a network would be a priority. She decided to apply for an internship with a big architecture firm. Against prevailing rules, she was hired as staff before her term had come to an end. She got to know the business and the people. Architecture was not her thing, but creating something beautiful out of nothing, and managing the process, was. Sarah knew that she had found her calling. Now she had to orchestrate her moves towards her goal. There were many opportunities: 'If you ever think of changing jobs, call me!' was a frequently extended invitation. She accepted twice, but only to learn more and expand her network.

Sarah became a feature in the world of the rich and famous. People who have money but no taste. People, who pay anything to show off the interior of their houses and apartments, but would fail any colour-blind test. People who had no interest whatsoever in keeping all that beauty in good order. That's where Sarah saw a business opportunity. Creating and preserving beauty.

It was at this juncture of Sarah's mulling that her body told her: time is up. I need a rest. She took a shower, went to bed and fell asleep right away.

Six

Jeremy was still wide awake. He would often have a nightcap with his friends at "L'Empereur", an old fashioned bistro on the corner of his apartment building, but tonight he decided otherwise. He preferred to savour a little longer the good feelings from his dinner with Sarah. Yesterday, the day of the accident, he had observed that Sarah was a beautiful woman. That was her *outside*. Tonight he had been offered a glimpse at her *inside* and he was intrigued by what he had seen. Jeremy was not easily shaken.

He had fallen in love a couple of times – his failed marriage was an extension of one of those occasions – but women were not his driving force. Yet, this Sarah-thing slightly unsettled him. Jeremy found it difficult to explain why he had decided to take care of her after the accident. In similar circumstances he would have scolded the person, beaten him (no, not her) up maybe or at least insisted on some form of compensation. Yesterday, it had been a totally different picture: one of compassion. Looking after her injuries had given him a feeling of purpose. Wanting to see her again and giving her a call in the evening had been a spontaneous emotion and action. Tonight's dinner with her had left him literally speechless, at times.

Jeremy stopped himself in his thoughts there. Asking himself questions, without having the answers was not new to him. In fact, his travels to foreign – and often exotic – countries had had a profound impact on his behaviour and beliefs. On the one hand, he had finely honed his survival skills and the physical capacity to defend himself against danger. On the other hand, he had become a "spiritual" person, someone who takes life as it comes and surrenders to the powers of the universe. Not expecting answers to questions was part of that trait.

Tomorrow night he would see Sarah again. This time it had been her initiative. She probably was perfectly capable of changing her bandages herself; nevertheless she had asked Jeremy to take care of her. Was the universe up to something? Jeremy did not expect an answer, but couldn't help feeling a sense of excitement.

And then also he went to bed.

Seven

When Sarah woke up the next morning she felt rather refreshed. Like Jeremy last night – but unknown to her – she also felt a twang of excitement about meeting up this evening. Now that she had broken her vows not to date anymore she felt comfortable with her decision to see Jeremy again. She was even more comfortable with the fact that it had been *her* initiative. That was the "old" Sarah, firmly in control of things, never mind her moments of confusion of late. Yes, those moments stayed with her during the day and the question as to "why" remained engraved in her internal circuit, but the prospect of meeting "this man" again was taking "pole position". Yes, Sarah was excited.

She had no difficulties in finding Jeremy's apartment on the Avenue des Princes. But this time, as opposed to two (only?) days ago she took her time to look around. It was indeed a magnificent building. The dimensions, architecturally, she found right, the sculpted gargoyles were beautiful and in good shape, but what struck her most were the bay windows, giving the exterior an almost human face.

She entered the main door and took the elevator to the top floor. She did not quite remember all the "geographical" details of her last visit to Jeremy's place, but there was only one door adjacent to the landing, so that must be his, Sarah decided. She rang the bell and noticed a brass nameplate under it: "de Besançon" it said.

Whatever, Sarah thought, and pushed Jeremy over as soon as he had let her in. She put herself on top of him, grabbed his manes with both hands, kissed him on his mouth and all over his face, tore open his shirt, removed his belt and lowered his trousers, took off her own blouse and pants, saddled him and fucked him royally.

'Wow', Jeremy exhaled when the hurricane had blown over. 'What was that?' Sarah was like a wilted leaf. Jeremy put his left arm around her shoulders, with his right one he lifted her hips and folded her gently against his sizeable torso. 'What was that?' he repeated. Sarah did not respond: she cried.

Jeremy put Sarah on his couch and set down next to her. She cuddled against him, still sobbing. Jeremy did not say anything, but felt pretty good holding this vulnerable creature in his arms and, to be honest, also about the sex they just had.

'Jeremy', she uttered through her tears, 'I don't know what is happening to me. I've never done a thing like this in my life. I'm so confused!' 'Never mind Sarah, everything will be all right', Jeremy tried to comfort her. 'Why don't you freshen up and have a shower. Then I'll see to your dressings and afterwards we talk.'

The shower did Sarah a world of good – she admired Jeremy's choice of tiles and fittings in his bathroom – , wrapped the clean towel that Jeremy had given her around her body and returned to the living room. Meanwhile Jeremy had opened a bottle of wine – red, but Sarah had no clue as to vintage or origin; she didn't drink, that's to say until yesterday –, and put some snacks on the coffee table. He handed her a glass: 'Cheers. I guess we've gotten to know each other a little better.' They clinked glasses and Sarah giggled: 'Yes, I think you could say that.'

Jeremy put his wine glass down: 'Now let's have a look at your injuries', and gently peeled the bandages away. 'That looks good. I think the wounds are healing well. I will put some more antiseptic and a few fresh dressings on them and you're out of the danger zone.'

While Jeremy went about his business Sarah again had this sensation of calm surrender, like two days ago when she was at his place and also, at moments, last night at dinner. 'Jeremy, why are you doing this? Why are you looking after me? You don't know me. You have no obligations towards me whatsoever, on the contrary: I owe *you*!'

Jeremy did not look up from his surgical duties and did not respond right away. Then he said: 'I don't know. Destiny? OK, I think we're done. Why don't you put on your clothes and we'll have a chat.' Sarah did as ordered, came back to the living room, set down in front of Jeremy's couch and took another sip of wine. 'Mmm, that's nice, what is it?' she asked in an effort to keep the communication light, to postpone the serious discussion that was looming. They had made love, no, they had had sex and she had - almost - raped him. There was some explanation to be done.

'Yes, that's a fine wine. I brought it up from my cellar this morning. Later I will tell you more, but first *you* speak. Tell me what you want to tell me, hide what you want to hide. I guess that you already know that you're safe with me. You have given me your confidence, letting me look after your injuries and letting your tears flow in front of me. Who are you and why are you in my house? And why do I think that I'm attracted to you?'

That last bit came out as a surprise to Jeremy. Emotionally, it might have been the truth, but mentally he had not worded that conclusion. It did not really matter, because Sarah did not react to the latter part of his questions.

Sarah sighed: 'Jeremy, I don't know. I don't understand what's going on with me and if I were to open up I wouldn't

42

know where to begin. Last night I told you the story of my childhood and the important role my father played during that period. I gave you a few titbits about my professional life. Other factual details seem trivial. But there is one thing that has hit me like a brick: I'm totally out of control! My behaviour of the last two days is testimony to that and, to tell you the truth, I'm scared. I've done some things, like drinking your wine, like accepting your dinner invitation, like having sex with you, that were completely beyond my intentions. I'm scared of the other things that might follow.'

She paused, her eyes staying focused on the wine glass in her hands. Jeremy looked at her. Once more he thought: she's beautiful, externally, but more importantly, in her vulnerability. He tried a lighter note: 'The dinner with you last night I found rather pleasant, the wine we're currently drinking I find delicious and the sex we just had I plainly found terrific. Life is not all bad.'

Sarah laughed, a beautiful and genuine laugh. She stood up and set down next to Jeremy. She put her arm around his shoulder and gave him a kiss on his cheek. 'Jeremy, I like you. Thanks for all you have done. Tell me something about yourself.' Jeremy sensed that Sarah was not yet ready to open up further and that sharing some private details about himself might expand the comfort zone.

'Well,' he started and took a sip of wine. 'My father was French. He is no longer alive and, honestly, I hardly miss him. In fact, I hardly knew him. He was in the shipping business and as a young man moved to Athens, Greece. That was where he met my mother. I was their only child. I adored my mother; she was so full of energy and ideas. As my father was always on the road, or rather in the air, I spend a great deal of time with her and we developed a great bond. That exists until today, although she got remarried and we hardly see each other anymore. My parents sent me to boarding school in the UK, but vacations I enjoyed with my mother. We both liked sailing and explored all corners of the Aegean Sea and other parts of the Mediterranean. Sometimes my father would be there, but most often not. It would just be my mother and me, and we were a great sailing team!'

'After boarding school I went to the London School of Economics. It was a trendy thing to do those days; not that it was my reason: I didn't know what I wanted out of life and a LSE degree could open many doors. While I was in London, my father was hit by cancer. I visited him a couple of times in the hospital and after he died I wanted to come back to Athens to look after my mother, but – strong woman that she is – she insisted that I finish my studies. I did stay in London, at least for a while, but did not finish my studies.'

'This is what happened: at the LSE there are many students from foreign countries. I teamed up with a man from Tanzania. His name was Kisyeri, but we all called him Kis. Kis and I became friends and he invited me to come and stay with his father during the summer break. His family lived in Arusha, close to Mount Kilimanjaro. I would miss my time with my mother, but she encouraged me to go and I did. And my life has never been the same again. Of course, life never is, but here you could really speak of a life-changing turn of events. I will tell you later what happened, but what about meanwhile grabbing something to eat?'

Jeremy looked at Sarah; she was still leaning against him, but he couldn't see her eyes and thus couldn't read her. 'I don't know', she said, 'maybe I should go home.' Both Sarah and Jeremy knew that she didn't mean it. This was a special moment, two souls meeting and being curious. 'I guess that's a "yes"', Jeremy replied for the two of them. 'We'll have a little something at the "Café du Théatre" and afterwards I'll take you home.'

Although she rarely ate out Sarah knew the Café. It was a "classical" bistro, with a splendid interior, high ceilings, crystal chandeliers, a beautiful choice of paintings on the wall (copied impressionists, of course), and waiters (no, no waitresses) who might despise you but nevertheless treat you like royalty. It was not for those reasons that Jeremy proposed the Café. No, it was the privacy this bistro offered, the spaciousness of the place; and then, it was, what you could call his "soup kitchen".

Before leaving the house, Jeremy called to announce his arrival: We will be two tonight.

Eight

They walked out of Jeremy's building; it was a balmy spring evening, full of promise, weather-wise that is. Jeremy took Sarah's arm and she held his tight, almost so as to avoid that he would run away. They talked about the things they saw, the architecture of the buildings, the awakening nature in the parks, the people, the traffic, things "neutral", that would not be food for arguments. It was not a long walk, ten minutes maybe, but ten minutes of "harmony" Sarah thought.

When they arrived at the Café, Jeremy opened the door for her. 'After you', he said, and let her pass. Then he moved in front of her to lead the way. Old fashioned gallantry, Sarah thought, what a blessing! 'Good evening, Monsieur de Bésançon, good evening Madam, your table is ready. Please follow me', the head waiter greeted them and, rather unnecessarily, escorted them to their table. He helped Sarah to sit down. 'Can I bring you something from the bar?' 'Yes, please, Fernando, the usual.' And for you? Madam?' 'Some sparkling water, please.' 'On its way', Fernando said and headed for the bar.

'I've been here a couple of times with clients', Sarah said, 'but do you come here often?' Jeremy laughed: 'That sounds like a worn-out pick up line. But yes, I do come here often. I don't cook, this place pleases me and when I'm in town I consider it my "dining room"'. 'Strange,' Sarah reacted, slightly changing the subject, 'three days ago I didn't know you. Since, I've been twice at your place and tonight you bring me to your dining room. Life certainly has its surprises.' And in between we had sex, Jeremy thought, but did not say.

The drinks were brought (Chivas for Jeremy - no ice -) and Sarah insisted on hearing the sequence of Jeremy's story: 'What happened in Tanzania?'

'I don't know whether I can give it to you in one go and I certainly don't want to monopolize our conversation. But before I give it a start, let's have a look at the menu, and if you feel like choosing for me: be my guest!' 'Oh no, let's not do that. This is your dining room. Tell me what's good and we'll go for it!'

Jeremy liked that: there was an equal-footing situation emerging, after an initial top-down anomaly. They went through the menu together: rather classical fare, no 'nouvelle cuisine', but a prominent selection of red meat. Red meat goes with red wine, Sarah thought to remember. Would Jeremy choose his wine first and then the food to match? She called herself to order: what a stupid question and who was *she* to come up with it? They ordered their food. Jeremy went for a beef fillet and Sarah for a tartare "coupé au couteau" and both chose a simple bouillon for starters. 'I don't want to make you drink, but I'll have a '98 Ermitage de Chasse Spleen to go with it. That's the wine we drank at my place.' 'I liked that one', Sarah admitted, 'but one glass only, not more. And can we now have your story?'

Jeremy obliged: 'I went with Kis to Tanzania, a country I had never visited before. I like discovering new places and I adapt easily, but Africa had not been on my radar. "Mud huts and poverty" my father had said and I never had taken the opportunity to prove him wrong. He was dead, but his death had not killed my curiosity. So, I accepted Kis' invitation. Kis' parents (his mother has since passed away) did not live in a mud house: on the contrary their place in Arusha was an old colonial mansion. When we got there I asked him questions as to the origin of the house. He did not have all the details, but gave me a few insights in the country's recent past: the German colonizers, the British, the first homegrown leader, Julius Nyerere. He also pointed at the majestic Mount Kilimanjaro, or where it was supposed to be, under a thick layer of clouds, and announced that we would be climbing that "mother mountain" as soon as the weather would allow us. "En passant" he wanted me to know that European wisdom was wrong in maintaining that Queen Victoria, ruler over what was British East Africa and now Kenya, had given the mountain to her grandson Kaiser Wilhelm II, ruler over what was German East Africa and is now Tanzania, but I guess I didn't care too much about that bit of historical folklore.'

'The house of Kis' parents had been built and lived in by Germans, but whether they had died there or gone back to Germany Kis did not know. His grandfather, although born a Masai, had lived among the Chagga tribe, that populates the eastern and southern slopes of Mount Kilimanjaro. He had become a wealthy trader in hides and skins and had moved to Arusha where he had bought the house. His grandparents had lived there until their death, but that was before Kis was born. I liked the house, its spaciousness and, in particular, its big veranda facing Mount Neru.'

'When Kis showed me my room I noticed a big piece of furniture in a dark corner. "What's that", I asked. "Some kind of piano", Kis replied. "My parents told me that it was there when my grandfather bought the house. There are other pieces of furniture as well. My parents never bothered to remove them and in fact we found some good use for some of those. Apart from the piano. Nobody plays, it just sits there."'

And then Jeremy went on to tell something about his youth. How his mother had inspired a liking for music in him. Not only Greek music, but everything. That he had, as a kid, played in various amateur groups. The piano had become his favourite instrument and his parents had enrolled him in an evening music school. It had been classical music but Jeremy had not particularly liked the rigidity of following composers' written instructions. He gave up the school; nevertheless his interest in music and in particular piano music remained.

'I recognize all of that', Sarah interjected, 'I went through the same process. But don't let me interrupt you, please carry on.' Jeremy did, as if he enjoyed reliving the past.

'I'll never forget. I approached the instrument, removed the blanket that was covering it and stood face to face with a beautiful horizontal piano, its black lacquer finish shining like a polished car. I opened the lid and touched some keys. The piano was terribly out of tune, as could have been expected. That was not a surprise, but what was: the name, in bronze lettering just above the keys, "Steinweg". I knew the name: a German house of piano makers for the most discerning clients, be they royalty or top concert musicians. The company's founder, Henry Steinweg, emigrated to the United States in the middle of the 19th century and changed his name to Steinway. The products of Steinway and sons have world-wide reputation, but his original instruments are still very much sought-after. And here this Steinweg was sitting, in this house, in this African outpost called Arusha. I tinkled some more, and was taken by the clarity of the sound. The soundboard was probably still intact. "How much do you want for it?" I asked Kis. "Nothing", Kis said. "Please take it away and free up some space for us." I couldn't have known at the time, but now, in retrospect, I think I do: "life" wanted me to take a different course.'

The food arrived and Jeremy stopped talking. 'What a story!' Sarah exclaimed. 'I would love to hear more.' 'But not now', Jeremy insisted. 'Let's eat.' They did and the waiter poured the Chasse Spleen. Sarah had more than the one glass she had intended to drink. She enjoyed the wine, but more importantly she enjoyed Jeremy's company. It had been a long time - ever? - since she had felt so good in the company of a man. Coming to think of it: it had been a long time since she had felt so good, period. Sarah did not want this feeling to go, and when Jeremy said, the food and wine having been duly consumed: 'It's getting late. I think we should be going', a sense of panic struck her; would she ever see this man again?

'Yes, you're right', she responded without much enthusiasm. 'We'd better get going, but yesterday you promised me that, if there was a next time, you would let me pick up the tab. So, let me pay.' 'Well, thank you very much', Jeremy acknowledged and waved at Fernando. Sarah settled the bill and they left the restaurant. 'Good night, Mr de Besançon, good night Madam. See you soon, I hope', the head waiter said and Sarah honestly wished that he meant "you" in the plural sense.

Jeremy took Sarah's arm again and this time she needed his support: the wine had made her a bit dizzy and her knees rather wobbly. They did not talk, both of them being in their own world of thought. When they arrived at Sarah's front door she heard herself speak: 'Jeremy, I had a wonderful evening. In fact the last few days have been rather special. I don't want this evening to end. Why don't you come up and I make you a cup of coffee.' What was she saying? she thought. Another one of those things she had never done before: inviting a man to her apartment. Before she could change her mind Jeremy responded: 'OK, with pleasure. But not for long. I have a busy day tomorrow.'

The coffee was never served; neither did Jeremy get to see much of her beautiful place. As soon as they entered her apartment they fell into each other's arms. It was not Sarah, who took the initiative this time; the happening was very much a mutual undertaking. They took their time; earlier that evening it had been a raw, animalistic, but most of all, short-lived emotion. Tonight there was tenderness and affection, bonding of the souls.

'Jeremy, you're welcome to stay the night', Sarah said, when they took a break at lovemaking, around midnight. 'I know that you have a busy day tomorrow and so do I. It's probably smart if we start our days in our own environments. But I would like to tell you something if you decide to go. I've been talking about my confusion of late and I'm not out of the woods. Far from it. It could quite well be that you have something to do with it. Right now, I will not ask you or myself further questions. I will try to take life as it comes and that includes you. I feel that you've become part of my life and I'm very happy with that..., I think. What I'm asking of you is that you don't consider this evening a one-night stand. I would love to see you again.'

Well, Sarah thought, I've said it, and with some precipitation realized that her discourse entailed a certain commitment. Was she ready for that? Jeremy took her hands and looked into her eyes: 'At least I owe you the sequel to the Steinweg story. Would you be free tomorrow night for that?' He didn't wait for an answer and kissed her on her lips. She kissed him back and Jeremy took that for a "yes".

Jeremy, maybe, had been the cool cat, the dominant character in the cast of the events of the last few days. But that was the surface. The encounter with Sarah had ruffled his inside and walking back to the Avenue des Princes he let his feelings flow freely. It had been a long time since he had told anybody the Arusha story or anything about his past, for that matter. He was now a successful commodities trader and in his business he had created an image as if he had forever existed as such. The fact that he had never gotten his LSE degree was nobody's business and, in fact, did not matter at all in his "milieu". He would tell Sarah the rest, or some, of the story one day, if not tomorrow.

But it was not Sarah that took front-row place in his mind when walking home; it was his past. He had gratefully accepted the Steinweg from Kis and he had wanted to do something in return. Kis' parents did not want to accept any money, but they were associated with quite a few projects that could do with a little help. He visited, with Kis, some of the rural clinics, open-air schools, artisan co-operatives, you name it. He was fascinated by the sense of purpose of those initiatives, and shocked by the meagre means, if any at all, at their disposal.

Jeremy got an idea: the Steinweg would certainly fetch a considerable sum in Europe. There were probably plenty of similar instruments or pieces of furniture lying about. Colonialists had arrived with their belongings and had left - if not died - without them. It was a matter of finding them, establishing the appropriate sales channels in Europe and keeping them supplied. The proceeds, after deduction of costs, would go to community projects where the artifacts had been found.

Yes, Jeremy climbed the Kilimanjaro with Kis. It wasn't a steep climb, but at almost 6000m oxygen is in short supply and breaking the journey in stages to acclimatize is recommended, so they had to take their time. It was the only item on Kis' and Jeremy's calendar which was executed as planned.

Jeremy did not return to London. He stayed in Arusha. Kis went back though, with instructions from Jeremy to find the most appropriate channel for selling the Steinweg. Kis did his homework and Jeremy took care of the logistics. The piano found its way to a happy new owner in Europe and with the proceeds of $15,000, minus costs, Jeremy made quite a few people happy in Africa. But had he done the right thing? For others, for him?

Jeremy arrived at the Avenue des Princes, number 312 and his thoughts returned to Sarah. What a woman! Yes, but why was he attracted to her? He wanted to fathom the nature of his feelings. What were they? Where did they come from? What was the obvious commonality in their individual existence, Sarah's and his?

Having entered his apartment, he picked up the phone and dialled her number. She answered, maybe expecting his call. 'Sarah, it's me. I'm sorry to bother you, but I need to tell you something. Tonight was an amazing night and I think that both of us sense that there is something special happening. I don't know what it is, but I'm rather excited and have difficulties with not knowing the sequel. Tomorrow will be a beautiful day; why don't we take advantage and have a picnic in the Ajuci. I know you have a busy schedule and so do I. But if I get up early tomorrow morning I can get quite a few things done and reschedule the other business into the remainder of the week. Maybe you would be able to do the same?'

Jeremy paused and Sarah did not react. 'If you say "yes"', Jeremy continued, 'I'll sleep like a baby and will be in sterling shape tomorrow!' Now Sarah had to say something: 'Wow, do I hear the freight train coming? All right, I'm game in principle, but please give me a call in the morning, so that I can confirm.'

That last bit was rather cheeky. Of course, Sarah had a busy day ahead, but "organizing" was her business and there was always Terry. Sarah would manage, she already knew. It was just that she did not want to *entirely* loose her skills in playing the hard-to-get game, certainly not after those unexplainable events of today.

Nine

They are called the Ajuci Mountains, but one should rather speak of a mountain range, a crest, pushed up by the earth's subterranean plates, a few million years ago, and having come to rest, so to speak, in the backyard of Sarah and Jeremy. It was a wonderful product of nature. Erosion had provided for gentle hills that accommodated farming, but generously had left numerous rocky peaks that rose to the sky like fingers of a hand. That's where Jeremy wanted to take Sarah. The Ajuci, which was only an hour's drive from the city, attracted many visitors, but most of them didn't get beyond the fast-food terraces "with a view". Only the discerning few left their cars and ventured with their backpacks into the "real thing". Jeremy was one of them, when he was not biking or travelling. Sarah was a less frequent guest and she did not recall when she had been in the Ajuci last.

Jeremy called around eleven in the morning: 'Hi, I'm set and the picnic hamper is waiting to be attacked. Shall I come and pick you up? Where are you?'

Wow, this man wants to be in charge, Sarah thought, and I don't mind. She had gone to her shop (why did she call it a shop? It was more the headquarters of a multinational enterprise) very early and there *she* had been in charge. She had established priorities, done what she could accomplish and left for Terry what she couldn't. Now she was ready for Jeremy and their outing.

'Good morning, Jeremy. I'm organized and ready. I brought my walking boots with me to the shop. So, yes, if you don't mind, please pick me up. The shop is at the Quai des Bergues, number 13. There is reserved parking behind the store, but if you give me a precise hour I will be waiting for you in front of it.' Jeremy knew the Quai des Bergues: 'Let's see. It's now eleven. I'll be there at eleven fifteen. I drive a blue Peugeot.' 'Done', Sarah replied and felt excited.

Jeremy arrived at the agreed hour. Sarah was waiting outside her shop (Jeremy did not know what kind of shop Sarah was running; he would ask her later), stepped into his car and off they were.

Sarah got a whiff of "couple" feeling: he was driving, she was the passenger. And she didn't like it; she didn't want to be part of a couple. She wanted to be Sarah, part of the universe, excluding exclusivity. Yes, she had a crush on Jeremy, she had admitted to herself before falling asleep last night (fortunately, she had concluded, after all she had made love to him). But she was totally unclear as to what to do with those emotions and couple stuff was not an option, at least not for now.

'Where are you taking us?' Sarah asked as soon as they had left the city. 'The Ajuci, if you're OK with it. I know a little plateau, which is a 45 minutes' walk up from the parking lot. It is a bit of a climb, but I think a jogger like you can handle it. The reward is stunning views all around.' 'Sounds good to me', Sarah responded, but the "couple" fear still lingered. They didn't talk very much during the car ride.

Neither did they talk very much during the hike. They admired nature in silence and filled their lungs with pure air. Jeremy was carrying the picnic stuff in a backpack (he'll probably have a first-aid kit in there as well, Sarah thought; let's hope we will not need it). They kept a steady pace with an equal rhythm (what a blessing, Sarah thought, no one-upmanship!) and after a final steep stretch reached the plateau. 'Wow!' Sarah exclaimed, 'this is beautiful!'

The plateau was a clearing in the forest, with thousands of spring flowers everywhere. In their joyful, tranquil presence they appeared to be in total harmony with the exuberance of the many little streams crossing the open space, which were jumping like a bunch of badly behaving children. All of that against a backdrop of tall rocky outcrops and uninterrupted views to the distant horizon. 'Beautiful', Sarah said once more. 'Look, there is herd of cows grazing. Jeremy, you did not exaggerate: this is stunning', and she planted a kiss on his cheek.

'OK, let's go to work', Jeremy announced matter-of-factly. He put down his pack and took out a blanket, which he laid next to a meandering stretch of an otherwise lively stream. He opened the hamper and started to "lay the table" with delicate efficiency. Jeremy had brought a selection of dried meats, cheeses, fresh vegetables and fruits (what a spread, Sarah thought, and what a connoisseur).

'But first things first', he announced. He pulled a thermos out of the pack, two glasses and filled those with white wine. 'Cheers, here's to you. Thanks for being here.' For a second Sarah was aware of her not-drinking habit, but she quickly put that thought away. She should surrender to this wonderful place and moment. A glass of wine wouldn't hurt.

They sat down on the blanket and started to nibble at the food. This is heaven, Sarah thought: total peace and tranquillity and what a blessing, feeling good in the company of another human being. She broke the spell: 'Jeremy, I'm dying to hear the sequel to your Arusha story.' 'You'll have it, but not right away. My senses are honed to the powerful presence of nature. The trees, the rocks, the water in the stream, us.'

Sarah took this as sign that Jeremy preferred not to talk and continued to eat in silence. There were plenty of thoughts going through her head, but again, she did not know what they were. Like two days ago, she had that marionette sensation: an unknown player pulling the strings. Again this paradoxical phenomenon: feeling at peace and confused, grounded and floating at the same time. What *is* this? she asked herself once more.

Without waiting for a response she pushed Jeremy on his back, threw her arms around him, buried her head in his neck and held him tight against her. She did not cry this time. Jeremy did plain nothing; he just let her. It was a strange sight: two adults laying entangled on a picnic blanket on a mountain plateau. After a while Sarah released Jeremy and rolled over on her back, spread her arms wide and laid there like a little angel, with her eyes closed.

What a beauty, Jeremy thought for the third time in so many days, but now he added something else: what an enigma! He did not want to disturb her, assuming that she was in thought. Instead he focused his antennae on the pine trees, the larches, the oak trees, the meadows, the grazing cows and all else nature was offering. This was his domain, his source of energy and equilibrium. But Sarah was still there as well; she had just made a gesture, which certainly had meaning. A meaning, which had not been revealed, but waited to be further explored.

He touched her lightly and she opened her eyes. There was a look as if she were surprised to see him, as if she had just woken up from a deep sleep. 'You're OK?' he asked and without waiting for an answer continued: 'You asked me for my story and I replied that I'd rather enjoy the beauty of the moment. Yet, this might be a moment to talk. Before we do so I would like to admit that I'm very much "man" and I see you very much as a "woman". We think and feel differently. I propose that in our communication we'll make room for that.'

Again Jeremy did not wait for a reaction and went on. 'The last few days we have spent time together in a rather intense and, if I may say so, unusual way. Neither you nor I know why it happened the way it did. Now, you're here, I'm here, that's all that counts. But could you please try to explain to me what happened to you just now?'

Sarah righted herself, put her arms around her knees and stared into the distance. She sighed and then began: 'I cannot give you a straight answer, because I don't have one. I got your message about the Mars and Venus thing and agree with your proposal that we recognize our male-female differences. If you have the patience I will, over time, throw out a few bullets and maybe by joining the dots we'll arrive at a clearer picture.

But I warn you, I'm as surprised about my behaviour of the moment as you have the right to be.'

She paused and reflected on what she had just said: "we" and "over time". There were "couple" connotations there! She turned her head and looked Jeremy in his eyes: 'I don't know what happened. Obviously, I don't throw myself on top of every man who crosses my path. In fact, I've never done a thing like that in my life and you can believe me! Why you and why today?'

'Let me try "today". This is a wonderful place and I think that I recognized the vibrations it transmits. I'm in particular in awe with those rock formations. They look so solid, so untouchable, so permanent. Something I might be craving for. Something that I would like to be and know I cannot be. Maybe I see you as my next best option: my rock. Clinging to you, instead of becoming one with those mountains. I know, that doesn't sound nice, comparing you with a piece of stone. I told you that I like you and once more: I'm grateful for all you did and enjoy being with you. But, at this point in time, at this very moment, I don't see you as a person, I see you as a mountain, an anchor.'

Sarah paused once more and turned her head away from Jeremy. Then, rather abruptly, looked him in the eyes again. 'You know, when I hear myself talk like that I get a glimpse of a certain truth. A glimpse, not more. My confusion and my actions of late, and now my comparing you with a mountain, there must be something there, some kind of connection, don't you think?'

Obviously, Sarah now wanted Jeremy to react, which he did. 'Thanks for being honest with me. What you're saying makes sense to me. I'm not a psychoanalyst, but my life experience has taught me quite a few things. You may indeed have arrived at a crossroad in your life, which happens to all of us at various intervals, whether we recognize it or not. Where I don't see clear though is this: I cannot at the same time be your therapist, your lover and your friend. These relationships have different levels of emotions and intimacy.'

'Our whirlwind encounter left also me with questions, but they are of a different nature than yours. I believe that, in a way, I've found my destiny, my purpose in life. Your presence fits into that, although in what role is not yet revealed to me. Hence, the therapist-lover-friend dilemma. What I've learned in life is to surrender, not to wish to control the uncontrollable. So, I'll let that dilemma rest and accept you in whatever shape or form. I propose that we accept the "coincidence" of our encounter and also accept the outcome thereof.'

Sarah looked a little puzzled: what was Jeremy saying? Had she put him off by comparing him with a mountain, creating a sentimental divide? Had Jeremy reacted accordingly with a wait and see attitude? Had she wanted him to go on his knees and declaring eternal love for her? What was Jeremy's meaning of "surrender"? Should she ask?

'I'm not sure whether I got your message', Sarah said, 'but it doesn't matter. One day you'll explain. Meanwhile I would like you to know that I'm enjoying the moment and your company.'

Is that all I want to convey? Sarah thought. No, but what else was there to say. She tried this: 'If you have no pressing engagements I would like to stay here a little longer, or maybe hike a little further?'

'OK, let's continue the trail and then return to the car via a different route.' Jeremy started to pack the hamper, folded the blanket and put everything in his backpack. 'Follow me', he ordered with authority. Sarah felt comfortable with that and had full confidence in Jeremy's skills as a scout. They walked for half an hour, Jeremy leading and Sarah following, without speaking a word.

They reached another plateau, now much closer to the rocky peaks. There were remnants there of what looked like a shelter for herdsmen, build, used and deserted in times long passed. Sarah leaned against a crumbled wall. 'Let's halt for a moment and admire the scenery', she proposed. Jeremy dropped his backpack and took position next to Sarah. He put his arm around her shoulders and she gently rested her head against his.

'You know', he said with his deep but soft voice, 'we talk about the five senses of a human: our capacities to see, hear, feel, smell and taste. There are some people who say that there is a sixth one: the sense of consciousness. That's what I experience when I'm in places like this one, the sense of feeling with my heart, the sense of unity with my environment, with the universe, if you wish. I first learned to recognize that sensation while travelling in Africa...'

Sarah would love to let him continue and hear the story, but something compelling overcame her: she took Jeremy's face in her hands and kissed him on the mouth; a warm, passionate kiss. Jeremy responded and when Sarah began to pull at his sweater and his pants he responded as well. In no time they were rolling in the grass, stark naked. There was an audience to witness their act of lovemaking: the birds, the trees, the mountains - the universe, as Jeremy had just called it – and 'it' seemed to approve with silent applause.

When the applause was over Sarah and Jeremy laid quietly on their backs, gazing at the sky above. Sarah was the first one to speak: 'Sorry to have interrupted your speech. What did you want to say about "consciousness"?' Jeremy grumbled: 'How can you feel sorry for something that gave us so much pleasure? I'd rather thank you, and very much look forward to more of the same!'

'Now, let's become a little practical: it's getting chilly. We should get dressed and head back. We've got a good hour to go before reaching the car. That will be around five. If you feel like it we could stop somewhere on our way to the city for a snack. Meanwhile I'll be happy to give you more of the Arusha story. Then I'll drop you off. I would like to do some work tonight. What do you say?' 'Fine with me', Sarah responded, still slightly trembling.

They put on their clothes and started their descent. Jeremy directed Sarah to a dirt road which led away from the stone hut. Ages ago it had probably been used to ferry supplies to and fro. Now, it looked as was in use for forest management and was kept in good order. It was certainly wide enough for the two of them to walk side by side. Jeremy locked his arm into Sarah's and started his "discourse": 'Sarah, for whatever it's worth, here comes the story. Not the whole lot, but the essential bit; that's to say, from *my* perspective.'

Sarah interrupted him again: 'Even if you make it all up, I'd love to hear it. And I love walking arm in arm with you, my "mountain"!' As if to emphasize her point she planted a kiss on his cheek. 'Now, if you would please be quiet for a moment', Jeremy protested. 'If not, I'll drop you right here and you can find the way home by yourself.' Sarah grinned, gave him another kiss and said: 'OK, promise.'

Ten

'Encouraged by the success of the Steinweg deal I went for more. I found plenty of stuff, not only pianos but all sorts of furniture, sometimes of extraordinary value. Yes, there were pieces damaged beyond repair, but there were many other items that, like the Steinweg, had been put away as odd, useless but precious remnants of a forgotten past. I had found a way of tracing them: I bought a flatbed truck, fitted it with a powerful bullhorn on the roof, hired local youths for song and dance and for announcing the purpose of my visit, and, like a modern-day troubadour, went on tour. "Cash" was the attraction and I paid generously for what met my taste. Like wildfire, word spread from village to village and often my truck was awaited with all sorts of artifacts displayed outside buildings and huts.'

'My logistics network started to develop gradually: moving the merchandize out of Africa into the hands of well-placed European dealers. I'll come back to that later, but will tell you now that Kis decided to step out. He was too busy with his studies. He had done an excellent job though and we're still friends. I cleaned out village after village, but I didn't feel guilty: after all this was European heritage and the money it raised – most of it – would come back to Africa and be put to a good use. And that, I discovered, was what I enjoyed doing most: working with cooperatives, small businesses, community groups and the like. People with vision, but often ill-equipped to turn their aspirations into reality. The ideas were honest and honourable; what was lacking were simple, but essential means - from buildings to pencils - and basic organizational skills. With "my" money I bought them hardware; my education, maybe more my intuition, provided the software.'

'I was acutely aware of my privileged position in those circumstances, and of the danger of becoming just a white guru, a "do-gooder". I knew that in order to make a difference I needed to become engaged and become involved, even if that would imply staying put for an undetermined length of time. And so it happened, I insisted on being part of the group and lived with them. We - the village elders, the committees, the administrators, the appointed managers, or just individuals, and I - got together to agree on goals and how to get there. Of course - let's not be naïve - "my" *money* was a prime mover, but as soon as my partners realized that I might have a "secret" to make that money "theirs" and make it grow, my *ideas* were listened to eagerly. And progress was being made.'

'While working on projects I continued searching for merchandize; after all, the pipeline needed to remain filled. As soon as I felt that my involvement in community activities had reached a degree of diminishing returns, I would get into the truck and move on. But not without having established a mutual commitment for the good cause. We're still talking about Tanzania here, but I had received signals of other African countries where there could be "Steinweg" business, so I moved on. I crossed the border to Malawi (with my bullhorn flat back truck; plenty of lessons there, but not for now), then to Zambia, to Zimbabwe, to Botswana and even to the tiny Kingdom of Lesotho.'

Sarah had been silent. Now she wanted to be part: 'Where is that, Lesotho?' 'In the heart of, and completely surrounded by, South Africa', Jeremy replied, without sounding superior. 'A country that, in my view should be declared a world heritage site. Its Maluti Mountains are probably the oldest on earth and should be respected accordingly. Human influence has let to disastrous erosion and provides another tragic example of how we can screw things up. But let me continue.'

Before doing so, Jeremy took a mental break for reflection: how he had enjoyed those years! Would he ever be able, verbally, to convey to other people, the intensity of his involvement with life's givings and takings, and his "discovery" of life's simplicity? Would Sarah understand? He was intrigued by the thought, but did not expect or desire an answer and simply continued his story.

'What I discovered also during my stay in Africa - I guess we're talking about a span of five years since I landed in Arusha - was the richness of African art, be it sculpture, jewellery, textiles, anything. Having run out of "pianos" I had to think of something else to keep the money flowing and an idea started to take shape in my head. I had been repatriating European furniture and had found a market for that. But it was technically only a matter of recycling. Why not exposing Europeans, and other non-Africans for that matter, to wonderful African art and giving Africans their dues and rewards in the process? I had seen the ebony wood carvings in Tanzania, the soap stone statues in Zimbabwe, the mohair tapestries in Lesotho, the grass baskets in Botswana and quite a few other gems. Yes, some of those items had already found recognition in the white men's world, but the rewards had gone to the middlemen and not to the creators. Why not use my "system" to bring change to that?'

'That became my next calling, not intentionally but evolutionary. I did not know much about "art", but I think that my mother had given me an eye for beauty. When I dug into this new challenge I discovered that quite a few merchants had been ahead of me and had spotted the uniqueness of African "handicrafts". They were also in the process of destroying it. They had encouraged their makers to mass-produce trinkets for European and American Christmas markets. The originality of the traditional designs was rapidly disappearing and what was worse: the craftsmen's talents, transferred from father/mother to son/daughter were in danger of being replaced by conveyer belt skills. An African heritage was in danger!'

'My mother's influence, most likely unknown to me at the time, made me see the difference between the true and the false and I now firmly decided to give my African adventure a turn. Why me? I had my network of connoisseurs in Europe and over the last five years I had found my way in Africa. With respect to the latter, I had learned a few Bantu languages, local customs and, very importantly, my way through officialdom and bureaucracies. So, I changed my tack, first in the countries I knew in Eastern and Southern Africa, later I added West Africa and finally trouble spots like Zaire and the Congo.'

'What I was looking for were not the already recognized (and often exploited) "stars"; no I was looking for the "source" of the art, be it Makonde in Tanzania, Shona in Zimbabwe or Kente in Ghana. Thanks to my Steinweg-prompted odyssey, I found those representatives of wonderful African creativity. I had to adjust my "formula"; yes, I would use my valuable sales network in Europe and the States, but my presence on the ground required adjustment. The artists needed to be left alone in exercising their craft; my role, I thought, was protecting them against exploiters, and seeing to it that in case of "commercializing" their works a fair return would accrue to them and their communities.'

'I made this my occupation for another two years and then life had something else for me in store. Unwillingly, I had become rather visible in many African countries and been approached by many shady businessmen and Government officials to enter into partnerships. I had refused. I had seen the corruption and the disastrous effects on the people of this beautiful continent. I didn't want to have anything to do with that. But, nevertheless, I had become part of this continent's rights and wrongs, and should not feel superior to my pars.'

'OK, that's perhaps a different subject, but what I'm telling you now is that I became exposed to some of Africa's other richness: the presence of what one – mistakenly - calls rear earth elements, the stuff that allows us to have mobile phones, laptops and space vehicles. Lanthanum, cerium and neodymium are a few of those. Most of those elements are mined in China, but also increasingly in African countries. Again, it is the poor man who is labouring long days for peanuts and the middleman and large corporations who rake in huge profits. I, or life, decided to get involved and now I own and manage some rare earth mines in Africa. Again, I'm ploughing my profits back into community projects around the working places.'

'You can imagine that by now I have quite a few things on my plate. To my regret I can no longer afford, like in the Steinweg period, to stay put for any length of time in the villages. To keep things going I had to come closer to the marketplace. I opened an office in London and for years I lived an ambulant life, shuttling between the world's economic centres, and of course Africa, until I finally got tired of that, and wanted to settle. And that's what I did six months ago, and that's where you and I, literally, bumped into each other. There you have my story.'

Eleven

They had arrived at the car by now. Sarah had not spoken, but once Jeremy had taken the wheel she reacted: 'That was quite a story I must say. Rather unusual.' She was thinking: he spoke so matter-of-factly. He must have felt very passionate about his undertakings, but there were no emotions when he recounted them. While I admire him for what he did, I'm not any closer to understanding him. What an enigmatic man!

She tried: 'Do you know where you go from here?' 'Not really. I've learned to live the present and that suits me. But I must admit that of late I'm asking myself questions. They are primarily of a relational nature. There have been women in my life and - I think I told you - I was briefly married once. Like you, I have had my disappointments in that area. Maybe I had the wrong expectations; maybe I did the wrong things. I don't know. I'm 45 now; maybe I *should* make plans for the future.' A bit of emotion, Sarah thought, that's better.

They remained silent until Jeremy stopped at the rest house he had talked about. It was off the road, hidden in the forest. A kind of lodge. Probably used by hunters and hikers, Sarah thought. The owner greeted them warmly: 'Hello, Jeremy, good evening Madam. So nice to see you! It has been a long time. Are you well?' 'Yes, James, I'm well indeed. Good to see you too. This is Sarah.' Sarah again got a whiff of this "couple" feeling, but now she didn't mind and on the spot she decided on a subject to be brought up during their meal.

'James, we would like to have a little bite, but before that, could you please bring us something to drink. The usual.' 'Would you like to have your drinks at the bar or rather go straight to your table?' 'We'll be at our table. Thank you.' 'As you wish. I'll bring you the wine.'

Strange, Sarah thought. Jeremy doesn't ask me what *I* want, whether I might wish to have a coke at the bar. I can see that he's a very independent person, and maybe that's the reason why he didn't last in relationships.

They sat down and James brought a bottle of Pouilly-Fuissé. Sarah glanced at the label: now that she had "surrendered" to participate in part of Jeremy's lifestyle, namely drinking wine with meals, she could as well become knowledgeable. After Jeremy had tested and approved of the wine, Sarah was poured a glass without having been asked whether she wanted any. It made her uneasy, but she did not protest. They toasted: 'Here's to a wonderful day', Jeremy said. 'Mmm, nice', Sarah responded, 'but again I'm drinking. You're a bad influence.' Jeremy only smiled.

This is the moment to attack, Sarah thought. 'Jeremy, I would like to come back to your story. In fact, I would like to come back to a whole lot more. Will you let me?' 'Be my guest, shoot', he replied and continued smiling, looking at her with those hypnotizing dark eyes. That unsettled Sarah, but she went ahead anyway: 'Look, this may not come out in any structured way. Yet, if I don't speak up I will torture my soul, which I don't want to do and I ask you to bear with me. Your story touched me, really, and - as you said - you may only have covered the essentials. Some day you may tell me more. And when I say "someday" I reveal that I expect that we will continue seeing each other. That's what I would like to bring up. I can revisit the last three days, our encounters and love makings, our discussions and our expressed thoughts. But I'm not from Mars. I'm from Venus. Let me not analyse things, or ask questions. I just would like you to know that I feel good with you, that I would like that feeling to last. Without trying to give that feeling a name, would you mind if I ask you...' Sarah hesitated, '...could we give our "friendship" a bit of structure?'

'Tell me what you have in mind', Jeremy reacted, still keeping his eyes trained on hers. Sarah dropped her head and studied her nails; she had felt uneasy with "couple" ideas, but she had also called Jeremy her "mountain", only a few hours ago. What did she want? More than ever she realized that she didn't know. And then she heard herself say: 'Jeremy, I want you in my life.'

They looked at each other in silence. Then Jeremy took Sarah's hand. 'We don't know where this is going, but what I've seen so far I like very much. Let's give it a shot.' Sarah felt both comforted and uneasy at the time. Yes, she had expressed herself, as she was accustomed to doing in her business. But the content of her message - I want you in my life - was rather unusual. What did that mean for her? For Jeremy? He had said "yes". What would be next? Love making had already taken place; what other glorious prospect could lie in store? The word "surrender", used by Jeremy—when was it, today, yesterday? —once more came to mind and Sarah wondered whether she should not take that route.

Jeremy woke her out her reflections: 'A few ground rules might be in order, though, and maybe I could propose one or two. Firstly, we have not talked about "love" and we may do so, if you wish, but only as a theoretical exercise. Secondly, unless otherwise decided, our independence will not be at stake.'

Those words are very Martian, Sarah thought and almost felt like running away. But then, Jeremy took her hands once more, his smile and eyes radiating and said: 'And I thank you for this gift, which you are and that the universe has bestowed upon me.'

When two people fall in love all is rosy. Nature is at work and closes a couple of internal circuits to mask reality. Sarah and Jeremy were not in love; fascinated by each other, yes; overflowing with warm feelings for each other, yes. But not in love.

When they drove back to the city, after the meal, they were in thoughts; each one reflecting on their own interpretation of reality. If an invisible thought reader had been a passenger on the car's back seat, he or she might have come up with something like this:

After three days of turmoil, Sarah and Jeremy had reached a station. Another plateau, if you wish, from where to survey the surroundings and to take stock of where they were in those. There had been magnetic attraction, indescribable and certainly irresistible. They had opened themselves up to questions, but had not insisted on answers. There was a hint of "relationship". Sarah had wanted "structure", Jeremy had insisted on "independence". Those words are not mutually exclusive, but not synonyms either. Sarah had professed goose bumps when thinking about relationships, yet she had called Jeremy her "mountain" and had profoundly said: 'I want you in my life'. Jeremy had admitted to disappointments in the relational domain. Yet, they had made a commitment, not necessarily to each other, but to life and to letting life run the show.

They arrived at the Boulevard des Fripiers. Sarah had wished that Jeremy would propose spending a moment in her apartment, but did not want to suggest that herself. She had taken enough unsolicited initiatives of late. It was not necessary either; Jeremy had another proposal: 'Tomorrow I have an early flight for a series of meetings in London. If you wish we can have dinner together once I'm back.' 'With pleasure', Sarah responded. 'I'll make dinner at my place. Give me a call once you've landed. Here is the code to my garage and the main front door', and handed him a card. 'Many thanks', Jeremy reacted, 'the garage I will not need. I'll take a taxi from the airport.'

He got out of the car, opened the passenger door for her, gave her a warm kiss and said: 'See you tomorrow'. And then he drove away and was gone.

Twelve

Sarah was very busy the next day. Terry had done a terrific job covering for Sarah, while she was frolicking in the Ajuci, but certain things Sarah had to do herself. There were a few projects on hand that had deadlines. One concerned the decoration of a stately home in the city, which had recently been bought by foreigners. Sarah had been contracted to furnish the house, before the new owners would move in. That would be in three weeks' time and a lot still needed to be done. It was not only the "furnishing", it was the whole caboodle: the colour schemes, the lighting, the sanitary arrangements, you name it. Sarah loved doing that, but she was dependent on the work and delivery schedules of others, and missing deadlines was not in her book. She had prepared the overall designs some time ago and today she would be running around to make sure that everything was being executed according to plan.

It was a good thing that she was busy, because she needed to free her mind of the events of the last few days. Jeremy had been very much in her head. No, not Jeremy; it was her "situation", her confusion and her strange behaviour of late.

Last night it had taken her a long time to fall asleep. Yes, the warm feelings for Jeremy were there and that was a pleasant sensation. But her own struggles had commended centre stage. How could she advance in a relationship if she were not in harmony with herself? Jeremy, her "mountain", might be of help, but it was ever so dangerous to rely on a partner for finding one's equilibrium. It would certainly create a situation of unequal footing. Should she seek professional help to get insight in her struggle? Would Jeremy consider that as a weakness? She had not come to any conclusion and instead decided to put the subject on the table over dinner.

And that had brought forward another subject: what would she cook for him, what would he like? What's exciting about starting a new relationship is the newness of it all: a first thing for this, a first thing for that. It would be the first meal she would prepare for him. It should be memorable.

And then she changed her mind: it would not be the last meal she would offer Jeremy. Why not begin with a simple concoction and build things up over time? Anyway, the composition of tomorrow night's dinner she had considered a minor issue. She would be plenty busy and have little time for shopping and cooking. That being settled, Sarah finally had fallen asleep.

'Hello, princess, I've just landed and am on my way. Barring traffic problems I'll be in front of your door, if not in your arms, in 30 minutes.' That was Jeremy's call at seven o'clock. There was no "how-are-you" kind of greeting, only authoritative bullets from a straight-shooting cowboy. He rang the bell at seven-thirty sharp. Sarah had showered and had selected a simple, but elegant dress for the occasion. She looked pretty, she had thought when making some final adjustments in front of the entry hall mirror. She opened the door and Jeremy, as announced, took her in his arms. He hugged her gently, kissed her on her cheek and whispered: 'You look great! I'm so happy to see you.' 'Me too,' Sarah replied truthfully, 'please come in.' She took Jeremy's coat and led him into the living room.

'Wow, what a place!' Jeremy exclaimed and strolled around to admire the furniture and the paintings on the wall. 'Sit down. Anywhere you want. I'll get you something to drink.'

Jeremy set down on the sofa while Sarah went to the bar. That had been a bit of a challenge today. Buying a bottle of whiskey was not difficult, but choosing wine was. She had asked the bottle store owner for advice: 'I'm preparing a meal for a guest who likes Bordeaux wines, but I would like to offer something else to surprise him. The main dish will be entrecôte with a Café de Paris sauce.' The shop owner had proposed a Chateau Neuf du Pape: 'It's a little less robust than a Bordeaux but it has a presence, a distinct fruity flavour that will nicely complement your entrecôte. May I suggest this one, a 1997 bottle of the Domaine du Vieux Télégraphe?' She had bought it without asking any further questions; that's to say not to shop owner. But she had two questions for herself: was she now becoming a regular consumer of alcohol, and would she now have to learn about wine? Not insisting on an answer on the spot, she had also bought a bottle of Mâcon-Chardonnay and a six-pack of Heineken, just in case.

Now, she pulled the white wine out of the fridge, poured herself a glass, filled a tumbler with whiskey for Jeremy and moved over to the sofa. 'Enjoy', she said while handing Jeremy his Chivas, 'and here's to us. Thanks for coming.' They toasted and the air started to fill with high-voltage emotional energy when they looked at each other's eyes.

Sarah had laid a fine table, after all that was part of her profession. But she had not overdone it; she had left the family silver and the crystal in the cupboard. There would be other opportunities to enthral Jeremy. Nonetheless, she had put some candles on the table. A little romance would be in order, Sarah had thought. Jeremy appeared to be comfortable in her place and Sarah could not help but asking herself: would this guy never feel uncomfortable, anywhere? After having finished their drinks Sarah suggested going to the table.

For starters Sarah had prepared a simple salad with foie gras. 'Delicious', Jeremy commented, after having finished his plate. 'Once more, thank you for being here tonight, coming to my place,' Sarah said, 'I have enjoyed our meals out, but for me there is no place like home. Like you, I travel a bit, but I need something I can call my own and this is it for now. Thank you for sharing this space with me. And now that I'm talking, there is something that I would like to bring up and have your views about. I don't want to monopolize the evening, nor spoil our meal, but I want to get it off my chest. What do you prefer: now or later?' 'Now!' Jeremy replied without a second of reflection. 'Then the main dish will have to wait', Sarah reacted and began.

'You remember what I told you, Monday night at "Chez Enzo". How I admired my father, detested my mother and regretted having lost contact with my brother. That's family stuff, stuff of the past. I also gave you some titbits about my private life of nowadays and heard me say things I did not know I had inside me. Yesterday I mentioned that I did not want to analyse my thoughts and actions. Nevertheless, today I did just that, and I'm not getting very far. I think that I need help from a professional. Before taking that decision I would like to have a second opinion. From you. But I warn you: don't play the father-child role. I will freak out right away. What I'm looking for now is some logistical support: where am I, where do I go and how do I get there?' Well put, Sarah thought, that sets the agenda and the boundaries.

'I hold my breath', Jeremy reacted half-jokingly. Sarah felt confident and comfortable. She did not quite know what she was going to reveal, what would surface from the depths of her soul, but something told her that with Jeremy she was in good hands.

'Let me start with telling you what I'm doing right now, professionally that is. Yesterday, you picked me up at my shop. I call it "shop", but it isn't, because I don't sell anything, that's to say no merchandize. I sell services and my shop is a kind of studio, depicting an image, an image of "beauty". You have not been inside and I hope you will one day. What I have created there, is my business card in 3D reality: look, this is what I can do for you. My clients are rich and, I'm sorry to say so, often idiots. Yes, I love my work - and will give some details later - and the freedom to exercise my profession, but off late I get this pearls-before-the-swine feeling. I design furniture: chairs, tables, cabinets, lamps, curtains, whatever I fancy. Whenever a client likes my stuff I have it manufactured. The design part I adore, but for myself; working for people with no taste, but lots of money, I don't!' Sarah paused, thinking about what she had just said.

'How long have you had this feeling of dissatisfaction?' Jeremy asked, to keep her talking. 'Oh, I don't know. It has probably been there for some time, but I didn't register it. I've told you about my confusion of late. It may be a signal from my subconscious self that something is amiss. That a fuse in my internal circuit has blown. Maybe what I've just told you about my work is an effect and not a cause. Maybe I have to start looking at my life as a whole, my childhood, my upbringing, my adolescence, my education, my career. Maybe I've taken a wrong turn somewhere.'

Sarah stopped and looked at Jeremy. Again she had this feeling of being totally comfortable with him. He was a friend, not a therapist, and now she was waiting for his views.

'I recognize a lot of that, the questions, I mean. I have had similar ones, and - as I told you - still have some, and will always have. I'm happy to give you more of my story, if you think that it might be useful. But not tonight. Let me say something else: first of all I would like to thank you for your confidence in me, for baring your soul, for disclosing your uncertainties in front of me, a man you hardly know. Secondly, while listening to you I decided that I don't want to be your therapist, but your friend. Yes, I offer you my ears to fill and my shoulders to cry on, but as a friend and I will refrain from unsolicited advice. You asked me a simple question: "Should I seek professional help?" My answer is:

"yes". But be careful: there are a lot of charlatans out there. Do a bit of research before you choose your "guru". And don't expect clear answers, or road maps. Let this person open your eyes for whatever may be hidden for you, nothing else.'

'Thank you, Jeremy', Sarah said and appeared relieved. 'I will look for someone. Thank you also for offering to be my friend. I will certainly take you up on your offer to listen to me when I feel the need to express myself. Now, let's have something to eat!'

Sarah disappeared into the kitchen, leaving Jeremy with his thoughts: Where am I going with all this, where does *life* want to take me? I'm pretty well satisfied with my life as it is. I have accepted life's challenges, offered my help wherever needed, have become humble and joined the needy, and received my rewards. Is my Karma not finished? Does life want me to do it all over again? What is the meaning of Sarah crossing my path? Am I called upon to be her "saviour"? Jeremy let it rest.

They had their meal, consumed in intimate togetherness. Their being together was all that both desired and after coffee there was only one possible sequence: spending the night in Sarah's bed.

Thirteen

The following days showed a pattern of repetitive behaviour: Sarah and Jeremy were working full days and during the evenings they had their meals together. Jeremy proposed a strenuous hike for Sunday - they both would be relatively free from chores - to the Pic de Série. It would be a daylong adventure, not entirely without danger. 'But the rewards are majestic', Jeremy had said. And they were. Both from the point of view of having uninterrupted vistas from the 3000m peak, and from accomplishing a common goal. At the top they embraced each other with an unspoken feeling: "If we can do this together, we can do other things, more plain, as well."

They had further discussions in follow-up to Sarah's confessions on Wednesday night, but there was an obvious desire to fully enjoy the here and now and that was experienced as totally sufficient. Was there a rosy fog, as in being in love? Maybe, but the question was not asked, neither was a response solicited.

And then - it was Wednesday again, ten days after they had first met - something seemed to give. After their Sunday climb, Jeremy had announced that he had to go for a business trip to Africa. It would be for an indefinite period of time and he had been rather vague about how he would stay in touch with her whilst he was in the bush. Sarah had asked for some kind of an arrangement, but he had declined.

The next days she had admitted to herself that she was looking at a big void. Jeremy had become a presence in her life and now he would be gone. Sarah was pointedly aware that Jeremy had to live his life and she her own. Nevertheless something had bonded them, even in this short spell of ten days, and she had grown attached to that feeling.

Hoping for some kind of last minute "clarification" she had invited Jeremy to dinner at her place the evening before his departure to Africa. His plane would only leave late afternoon the next day, so that would give ample time for moments of togetherness. Yes, it had been a wonderful evening: the feelings, the food, the wine, the sex. Sarah would be the last one to deny the pleasures she experienced. "Love" was still an unspoken word, but, if the feelings are there, who cares about words? And then, without providing "clarification", Jeremy had walked out.

Fourteen

'Sorry, I can't stay', was all he had said before walking out of the door. Sarah woke up, still lying on the couch. Reality hit her hard: Jeremy had left her. It was four o'clock and she knew that she could not fall asleep again; she was too upset. She was punishing her brain with looking for clues for his sudden departure, but could not come up with any. In spite of the nightly hour, she decided to call Jeremy; she would insist on getting an answer as to why. She had the *right* to ask for and be given an explanation.

She dialled his land line: no answer. She dialled his mobile: no answer. She thought of going to his apartment, but decided against it. That would be too self-depreciating. What else could she do? Going back to bed, she had already ruled out; instead, she decided on getting busy and starting her working day. But before doing that, she would send Jeremy an e-mail. He had given her his address and although she had never used it, this now might provide a lifeline.

'Dear Jeremy', she started. She reflected for a moment: was that a proper opening after what he had just done to her? Never mind, she decided and continued: 'It is not my intention to enter your private space, but I need to get something off my chest, lest I go crazy. Your coming into my life has had a profound impact on me. I am not aware having experienced anything like it. I will not further elaborate because I know that you know. I believe that there was a mutually felt sensation of bonding. Now, all of a sudden you broke that bond. I think that I have the right to know: why? Life has its incomprehensible ways, but if we are to progress in life, which I'm committed to do, I would like to understand. Can you please tell me: what happened? Sarah.'

She reread her message and was tempted to write more. To say all the things she hadn't said during the last ten days, to admit emotions she had felt, but had refused to express, to admit her vulnerability and to demand Jeremy's support; but she didn't. For now, her priority was simply to stay in touch with Jeremy. After she had pressed the send-button Sarah felt a little better: she had acted. The ball was now in Jeremy's court. She took a shower, got dressed and went to her shop.

The first thing Sarah did after arriving was switching on her computer: just in case Jeremy would respond. With all her will-power she started to plan her day. Creative stuff was not an option, planning and organizing was probably a better choice. The last ten days she had not spent the usual 12 hours on her job. Jeremy had been a priority in her schedule and other chores had taken a back seat. There was some catching up to do and that would take her mind of Jeremy. Or so Sarah thought.

It did not happen. Yes, she took a stab at the business at hand, but failed to concentrate. The thoughts raging through her head almost paralyzed her and completely took over the functioning of her system. She had to sit down from time to time to catch her breath, or rather to force herself to breath. There was a sense of panic, of total disorientation, of having lost all reference to life's bearings. There was no left, no right, no up, no down, no reason, no purpose. Sarah was lost and the only person who could help her finding her way out of this labyrinth was Jeremy. Jeremy *had* to come back. Sarah was aware that before Jeremy had appeared on the scene she had not been her usual self, but that was another story. "Life" had offered her Jeremy to help her solve her problems. And now "life" had taken Jeremy away. She would not let that happen: Jeremy *had* to come back.

Why had he left her? Had she in anyway offended him or hurt him? Yes, there had been moments when she had wanted to be in control, like most of the time when they had sex, but Jeremy did not seem to mind. She had refused to be lectured at, but Jeremy had no inclination to impose his views. Their moments together had been pure bliss, for her – and she was sure – for Jeremy. There had been no reference to a common future, but Jeremy had clearly expressed a commitment to accepting the present, with all its consequences. What could possibly have gone amiss? In her emotional haze Sarah would not be able to provide answers to those questions: Jeremy would have to do that. She took her mobile and dialled his number. There was no answer. She sent him an SMS: 'Jeremy, please call me before leaving town.' Jeremy did not call.

It was eight o'clock and Terry walked in. 'Hi, Sarah, you're already here?' she said by way of greeting. Terry noticed immediately away that there was something wrong: 'Sarah, are you all right?' Sarah looked away and mumbled: 'No worries. I'm fine.'

Terry put herself in front of Sarah and took her by the shoulders: 'Listen to me. We've known each other for quite some time. Off late you seem to have changed. And more recently – say the last few weeks – I feel that you have become distant. Please, don't misunderstand me: it's no criticism. You know that I'm fond of you and that I love working for you. But seeing you in such a state pains me and I insist that you tell me what's going on!'

Sarah remained silent, still staring at an unidentified object. Then she looked at Terry, put her arms around Terry's shoulders and started to cry. It was another of those watersheds, an explosion of tears accompanied by airbursts, exhaled and inhaled by the body at irregular intervals, locked together like braking surfs on a windy beach.

After Sarah had calmed down she started to talk. Last week she had hinted at Jeremy's existence, but not given any details. Now everything came out: how they had met (Terry was aware of Sarah's accident), their outings in the mountains, their dinners and, for the first time, Sarah admitted that she had fallen in love with him. 'And now he has left me without explaining why. He does not answer his phones and this afternoon he will fly out to Africa for I don't know how long. I'm totally devastated. I don't know what to do!' 'Have you had breakfast?' Terry asked. 'Shall I get you something?' 'No, thank you. I'm not hungry', Sarah replied.

Terry did not know what to do. Counselling was not her forte. Yes, she could listen, but there was something else. The Jeremy story had exploded ten days ago. Terry had observed that Sarah had changed weeks, maybe months before then. Was Jeremy's sudden departure the full story or was there more?

Terry set Sarah down on the chair in front of hers. She began: 'Sarah, I'm terribly sorry for you. I cannot possibly know why Jeremy left you. I can imagine that *you* would like to have an answer to that question, but that might not be forthcoming, at least not now. What I see are challenges of two different dimensions: short and long term. Of immediate concern is your recovery of the shock which you experienced today. Maybe I can help you with that and if you so wish I could propose a few things to distract your mind. Longer term: it might be helpful to get professional help from someone who can assist you in getting a handle on the bigger perspective. I could help in doing a search for a reputed counsellor.'

Sarah listened, but only partially. What she wanted right now was a magic trick to bring back Jeremy, her "mountain"

Terry went into action mode: 'Now, let's look at your schedule for today. At nine o'clock you have a meeting with Lady Greenwood. She will come here to look at fabrics for her curtains. I propose that we reschedule. I'll call her and think of some excuse. At eleven you have an appointment in town with the Barclays for the Sarassin project. We could advance that and then I'll take you for lunch at the "Jacaranda". You had asked me to block the afternoon for design work, but you might not be in the mood for that, so we could go and visit some galleries. I understand that there is a new artist at La Fontaine. We could also do a matinee at the "Hameau". I read some good reviews about the play that's running. What do you think?

'Fine with me', Sarah replied meekly, at the same time wishing for her mobile phone to ring. 'OK, that's settled then. Let *me* be in charge for a change. Help yourself to a cup of coffee, while I make some calls.'

Sarah was in a haze. The oddness of the situation – Terry in charge, rather than she, Sarah – was not the reason; she hardly registered it. It was this overwhelming feeling of *total* abandonment that paralyzed her. A sentiment of moral and emotional amputation. Something she had never felt before and could not give a place. She sat down, buried her face in her hands and started to cry again.

Over lunch at the "Jacaranda" Terry tried to make her talk. Sarah's story was rather incoherent and contained more questions than facts. Terry had difficulties in getting some kind of picture, as Sarah failed to string the beads together and insisted on exclaiming: 'Why did he do this to me?' Of course, Terry had no answer, but she became increasingly convinced that Jeremy was *not* the issue, that she, Terry, was sitting in front of a different Sarah than she had known. They had lunch together frequently; today was the first time that Sarah had ordered wine. Not one glass, a whole bottle.

Terry did not want to comment. If there were big issues at play: that would be the game of the pros. She had called a few friends earlier this morning and discreetly enquired about counselling options. She would follow through with the information that had been given. Sarah deserved her help, she strongly felt. Although she was fond of Sarah and considered her a terrific boss, Terry had never thought of Sarah as a close friend. But now there was a situation: close friend or not, here was a human being in terrible need of help right now and, apparently, Terry was the only person present to extend a helping hand. 'Tell me once more how you and Jeremy met', Terry tried.

Sarah sighed. Ten days ago she could not have predicted the agony of today; reliving the moment of her encounter with Jeremy and the blissful days that followed might provide some emotional relief, even make her believe that the events of today never took place and were only a terrible nightmare out of which she would soon awake.

She began: 'I was jogging as usual on Sunday morning, but somehow I lost my way and crossed the bike trail. I didn't see a cyclist coming and we crashed.' I know that part, Terry thought, but did not say anything. Sarah continued to repeat what she had told Terry just a few hours earlier: that she had gone to Jeremy's house and how he had treated her injuries. That Jeremy had invited her for dinner and that he had subsequently organized some mountain hikes.

'Did you make love?' Terry wanted to know. Sarah hesitated. They had had sex, they had made love. When was the first time that she had recognized *feelings*? She recalled her rather "spontaneous" behaviour on Monday night when she had entered Jeremy's apartment and virtually raped him. That was a "detail" she did not feel like sharing with Terry. Instead she said: 'Yes, we did. Almost every day and it was wonderful.' And she burst out in tears again. 'I was so sure that he loved me', she said through her sobs.

'What does Jeremy do?' Terry asked to change the subject to something less personal. Sarah did not go into the Steinweg story and simply said: 'He's a commodity trader. You think there might be something wrong with his phone?' 'He probably switched it off', Terry replied. 'What do you think happened?' Sarah insisted. 'I have no way of knowing', Terry answered. She had had her share of emotional turmoil, but was now living with her partner of fifteen years. Her "love life" was pretty stable. 'And you may never find out', she continued. 'I don't think it is important. What *is* important is to protect yourself from further suffering. *Not* to torture yourself with questions you can't answer, or with creating imaginary scenarios, past or future, in your head. That's useless as they always will be imaginary and thus false. Try to lift yourself out of your darkness with things that give you pleasure. Life will do the rest.'

Terry was painfully aware that Sarah was lost. It saddened Terry; she was fond of Sarah and had an enormous respect for her resourcefulness and her organizational skills. Now, the woman in front of her was in pieces. What could she do to help?

She moved her chair and put her arm around Sarah's shoulders. Sarah, now crying softly, leaned her head against Terry's. There were other guests at the "Jacaranda", but these two women were totally oblivious of their environment. There was a "situation" here, a situation that had a right of way, a natural priority over anything else, and everybody appeared to accept that: no prying eyes, no pointing fingers, no interfering waiters. There was raw, unadulterated agony for everyone to see, but to be left alone.

After ten minutes (or was it ten hours – who was counting?) Terry said: 'I think we should be going. Let me ask for the bill.' Sarah dried her eyes and the two women silently left the restaurant. 'I would like to go home', Sarah said as soon as they were on the sidewalk. 'Thanks for being there for me, for lunch and for having proposed a programme for this afternoon. But now I feel like being alone. Please drop me off at the shop and I will see you tomorrow.' 'As you wish', Terry replied.

Sarah did not go home, she went to the airport. The city airport was pretty small, with only one departure hall. Sarah set down, watching passengers hurrying to the gates. She stayed there until the last plane left. Then she got up and returned to her car. She had not seen Jeremy.

Fifteen

Jeremy had *said* that he would take a late afternoon flight, but he had departed early morning. After arriving at Heathrow he had taken a taxi to London where he made a few business calls. Then he returned to the airport and boarded a BA plane to Dar-es-Salam, where he would arrive early the next day before taking a connecting flight to Arusha.

Jeremy had travelled a lot and had trained himself in adjusting his body rhythm to travel schedules. During night flights he would order a whiskey, skip meals, cover himself under a blanket and sleep until the "wake-up call". Tonight he had his whiskey and blanket, but sleep did not come. His sudden departure from Sarah's apartment had been a conscious decision, but had not left him unaffected. Had he taken the *right* decision? He believed he had, yet he missed Sarah terribly. After all he had spent ten days, without interruption, in her company and those had been very intense days. What a woman! he admitted once more before fatigue set in and he finally fell asleep.

Kis' father was waiting for Jeremy at the Kilimanjaro International Airport, near Arusha. Jeremy was very fond of the old Masai and whenever he could, would make a stopover in Arusha to spend time with him. 'Habari gani, Mzee', Jeremy greeted him, 'how are you?' and hugged him warmly but respectfully. Jeremy always called him 'Mzee', although he knew quite well that this was an honorary title, reserved for the elderly, rather than his name. They drove to Mzee's house where Jeremy would spend the night.

Some time ago – it was before Sarah – Kis had called Jeremy: Mzee had an idea, but needed help and Jeremy was the right person to give it. This was the story: some 80km east of Arusha is a place called Moshi. In colonial times Moshi was the centre of rich agricultural plantations, primarily sisal. When synthetic fibres began making inroads, the plantations fell into disuse, with disastrous consequences for employment. A number of projects to replace sisal were launched, with mixed results and the authorities of Moshi were eagerly looking for investors to prime the employment pump. Ideas were there, but execution was the challenge. Mzee – now living in Arusha, but still feeling emotionally attached to Moshi, where his father hailed from – was one of the originators of ideas. In Arusha he had seen foreign investors grow tropical vegetable hybrid seeds for export. When travelling to neighbouring Kenya he had seen massive flower nurseries for export. Could Moshi not do the same?

Mzee, as his "title" implied, was a wise man and sensitive to the motivations of investors: money. The investors would come, make money and if the money were no longer there, they would go. Mzee wanted something anchored in the local economy and society. No stop-go, go-stop type of undertaking, but something that could grow and evolve. He himself was now too old to get involved in major business undertakings and seeing the end of his days approaching he had given Kis a call: 'I have something for you and your friend Jeremy to sink your teeth in', and had offered Kis a vague idea of what he was toying with. 'Father', Kis had replied, 'I'm terribly busy with launching a new venture in London, but I'll promise you that I will approach Jeremy.' And he had. 'All right', Jeremy had said, 'I will look at it, but not right now. I have quite a few projects on my burner that require my attention. Once I find a slot I will travel to Arusha and talk to Mzee.' And thanks for the Steinweg, Jeremy had thought, being gratefully aware that this piano had led the way to his fortunes.

'Look, young man', Mzee started after he had set down Jeremy on his veranda and had served him a whiskey (it was not even midday, but Mzee knew that Jeremy did not live by sundowner rules). 'This is what I have in mind. The Moshi City Council has offered me a freehold lease on a large tract of land, close to the Kilimanjaro. It's an old, dilapidated sisal plantation, deserted by its British owners and subsequently repossessed by the Nyerere Administration. I would like you to investigate what we can grow there. I'm thinking of roses; not the supermarket variety as they do in Kenya, but the exclusive, long-stemmed hybrid Tea Rose variety. I've been told that Europeans pay a fortune for those things and in your network of luxury lovers you can certainly find some takers.'

'But that's not why I approached you and Kis. I know about your work and admire you for what you've done: helping people to help themselves. My project is about that: I want the flower growers to be the owners of the nurseries. I want houses for the workers, schools, clinics, utilities, roads, you name it. I want it to work and I also want a fallback arrangement in case it doesn't. What I'm asking of you is to come up with a plan, discuss it with me and the authorities. Once approved, I would like you to supervise its execution and stay on board for as long as necessary. You don't have to do it for free; fix your fee as you see fit. I have arranged for a meeting with possible stakeholders to be convened by the Mayor of Moshi tomorrow morning.'

Mzee stopped there and took a sip of his whiskey. It was not his habit to drink alcohol, but when Jeremy was around he gladly made an exception. 'Cheers', Jeremy said, and thought: that's what I like about Mzee, strait to the point, no bullshitting. But, what a challenge, this project.

'Mzee, thanks for thinking that I may be useful. I don't make promises, but one: I will gladly work at your proposal and meet with all parties concerned. I will move to Moshi and stay there until together we have agreed on the feasibility of your project. Where it comes to its execution: we'll talk about it when the time is right. Once more, cheers, to the success of your project and to us!'

And then Sarah entered Jeremy's mind. He had hinted at leaving for an indefinite period of time, now he had committed himself to Mzee. There was no way back, at least not for now.

110

Sixteen

When Sarah got home, she was a wreck. The hours of waiting, in vain, for Jeremy at the airport had sapped the last drops of energy from her already drained reservoir. Aimlessly she paced through her apartment, recalling or trying to recall precious moments spent there with Jeremy, unto only 24 hours ago.

Jeremy's bottle of whiskey was still standing on the bar shelf. Intuitively Sarah felt that he would never come back to drink it; she could as well pour the whiskey down the sink. No, she would take revenge on him: she would drink it. She took a big gulp, straight from the bottle. And another. She just made it to the couch and then she collapsed.

Sarah was awakened by her telephone, at ten in the morning. She was dizzy and sick, but the thought that it could be Jeremy gave her an adrenaline boost and she answered. It wasn't Jeremy, it was Terry: 'Sarah, are you well? I'm worried.' 'No, Terry, I'm not well', Sarah replied rather unnecessarily, but omitting the explanatory whiskey detail. 'I'm not coming in today.' 'I'm sorry to hear that. Is there anything I can do?' Sarah did not reply. Reality hit her once more: Jeremy had left her and the agony of yesterday now had the company of a furious hangover. 'Sarah, are you there? Do you need help?'

Terry insisted. 'No, thank you. I will probably rest some more. Then I'll see.'

Terry did not give up. Sarah was not the character to succumb to adversity. As long as Terry had known her, Sarah had always, or almost always, dealt with challenges, big and small, in a determined and forceful manner. Now Sarah sounded like a weakling, a beaten dog, like someone who had lost the will to fight.

Yesterday afternoon Terry had made progress in finding a counsellor and managed to talk to a certain Dr Lemaire – a reputed psychologist, according to friends – over the phone. She had described what she had noticed in Sarah's behaviour of late and, in particular, of yesterday. Dr Lemaire had not wanted to discuss the matter – that's between the patient and me, he had said – but had agreed to see Sarah, if she so wished. 'But not right away', he had cautioned, 'my calendar is booked solidly for the next few weeks.' 'Doctor', Terry had pleaded, 'I'm terribly worried. Is there a danger that Sarah would inflict some permanent damage onto her?' 'Not necessarily', Lemaire had replied. 'You describe her as a strong woman. She may suffer now, but not lose her mind and do stupid things. I will call you if there is a cancellation in my schedule. Meanwhile, try to encourage Sarah to find comfort with her friends.'

After Terry hung up she wondered: who are Sarah's friends? Sarah had never talked about her friends and her off-duty activities, like sports, were solitary affairs. Would she, Terry, be her only friend? A scary thought, but Terry decided there and then that she would look after Sarah until Sarah would be able to look after herself again. That's why she didn't give up, didn't take "No" for an answer when Sarah refused help.

'OK, you rest. It's ten o'clock now. I will cancel your appointments for today and take care of the business, as best as I can. In the afternoon I'll come over to your house and bring something to eat. Meanwhile don't move! Promise?' 'Promise', Sarah replied and switched off her mobile.

Sarah tried to sleep some more, but didn't succeed. She went to her medicine cabinet to look for some aspirin to fight off her headache. When she held the bottle in her hand, there was a little voice in her head saying: 'Take the whole bottle and your agony will be over.' 'Never', Sarah said aloud, as in response, 'Jeremy is not worth it.' But the presence of the thought, even for a split second, scared her. I have fallen deeply, she admitted to herself, and I fail to see the hooks to enable me to lift myself out of my hole.

She took a shower, but did not get dressed. Instead she put on her robe and opened her computer, desperately wishing for an e-mail from Jeremy. There was none. Would he have read hers? If Jeremy had left on a business trip, he would certainly want to stay in touch with his office and check his mail? But what if he had not left on a business trip? He had not been at the airport; what if he had just taken his bike and disappeared into the mountains? Would he read his mails?

Sarah recognized her confused state of mind and the futility of trying to find answers to those questions. She would just write to him; one way or another her message would reach him. 'Dear Jeremy', she started, 'you have not replied to my previous mail. There is obviously a reason, but unknown to me. What I *do* know and what I want you to know as well, is that your departure has been a shock to me and has thrown me in a deep black hole. You're the only one who can help me to get out of it. Please send me a sign of life.' Sarah stopped there. Her last e-mail had ended: 'With all my love.' What would she say now? She settled on: 'I'm thinking of you. Sarah.'

Then she saw herself pick up her mobile phone, dial a number and heard herself say: 'Hi, Jacques, it's Sarah. I would like to talk to you. Are you free for drinks tonight? Great. Six o'clock at the "Café du Théâtre"? Fine, see you there.'

What had she just done? Sarah wondered. Jacques was her last lover, a man she had left a year ago. Why would she want to talk to him? And what had prompted her to dial his number without the slightest premonition?

Seventeen

Jeremy had planned his departure for Arusha carefully: he had anticipated decisions and actions to be taken in the weeks ahead and had given instructions to his associates and staff to do the necessary. He had convened board meetings in London to ensure that immediate corporate actions were firmly aligned with his vision. He had announced that he would be gone for an indefinite period. 'I can be reached by phone or by mail', he had added, 'but only for extreme urgencies.' And then he had boarded the BA flight.

Only after Jeremy had unpacked his bag and showered did he switch on his iPhone. Of course, he knew that Sarah had tried to reach him by phone and on purpose he had not answered. He had also read her first e-mail. Now he saw her second one. He had expected it, yet the level of distress it contained aggrieved him. He had no intention of replying, but he tried to visualize Sarah in her situation. He had seen her "outside": the independent, successful businesswoman, he had also been allowed to see part of her "inside": sensitive and vulnerable. He could imagine, almost *feel,* her sufferings. He felt for her, but he would not reply.

Eighteen

Terry had a key to Sarah's apartment. During Sarah's lengthy periods of absence Terry would come in to water the plants, empty the mailbox and, in general, orchestrate the "make-believe" that the apartment was lived in. Terry had taken the key, but nevertheless rang the bell when she arrived with a few sandwiches. Sarah opened the door, still in her robe: 'Come in', she welcomed Terry without much enthusiasm. Terry looked at Sarah; what a mess she thought. She entered and right away noticed the half-empty bottle of whiskey on the table. She pretended not to see it and instead moved into cheer-up mode. 'Hi, I brought something to eat. If you don't mind, I will join you. Any milk in the fridge? Let me have a look.' Terry put placemats on the table, found plates, cutlery and glasses, unpacked the sandwich box, poured the milk and said: 'Lunch is served. Let's eat!'

Sarah set down at the table, but did not touch her food. 'I'm not really hungry', she said. 'Come on, you must eat', Terry tried to encourage Sarah and took a bite of her sandwich.

Before coming to Sarah's she had decided not to bring up the subject of Jeremy; she would just listen to what Sarah wanted to say. But the moment she was about to leave the shop Lemaire's secretary had called: there had been a cancellation and the doctor could see Sarah next Monday at four o'clock. 'I will talk to her and let you know this afternoon', Terry had promised. So, that issue has to be brought up, but not right away, Terry thought. Instead she talked about the business, who had called and what she had replied.

Sarah hardly listened, not looking at Terry when she spoke. She nibbled at her sandwich and put it down again. She didn't drink her milk. Terry tried again: 'Madame de Fontebleu came in this morning. She is moving to the Beau Rivage and wants you to do the renovation. She gives you a free hand.'

Sarah straightened her back, looked Terry in her face and with a forceful blow of her right hand swiped the full glass of milk off the table. It fell in shatters on the floor, spilling its contents in all directions, including on the wall, where they found company of the traces of beer, which Sarah had deposited there, with similar force, only a day and a half ago. 'That's what I do with a free hand', Sarah shouted and ran towards her bedroom. She slammed the door behind her.

Terry stayed at the table, bewildered: what was going on? What was she to do? She could hear Sarah crying in her bedroom. Should she go in?

Terry decided to wait and meanwhile reflected: Sarah's condition, whatever it was, was *totally* beyond her control.

Lemaire would have to deal with that. Meanwhile she would try to protect Sarah against herself. She picked up the bottle of whiskey and poured its contents into the sink. Then she entered Sarah's bedroom.

Sarah was lying on her belly, her head buried in a pillow. Terry tiptoed towards her, stretched out next to Sarah on the bed, and put her arm around Sarah's shoulders. She also buried her head in a pillow and softly cried with Sarah.

It was late afternoon when they both got up. There was a sense of calm, stillness after a storm. 'Thank you, Terry, for being with me', Sarah said. 'Thank you for all you've done. And I'm terribly sorry for my behaviour. I don't know what's happening to me, but I sincerely apologize for making you part of my misery.'

'Don't you worry', Terry reacted, 'that's what friends are for. And I've got news for you. I received a call from Lemaire's office this morning. He is a highly recommended counsellor and he can see you on Monday. What are your plans for tonight?' 'Thank you for arranging that. Yes, I agree, I need help. Tonight I have an appointment with an old friend. Once more, many thanks for all you've done. I'll see you in the shop tomorrow morning', Sarah said and let Terry out the door.

122

Nineteen

It was quite a gathering in Moshi: the mayor, the Kilimanjaro Regional Commissioner, a couple of city councillors, some key representatives of the farming community, the president of the Kilimanjaro Chamber of Commerce and the Permanent Secretary of the Ministry of Agriculture and Cooperatives, who chaired the meeting. He conveyed to the assembled group that he had received authority to also act on behalf of other Ministries and the National Development Corporation. Mzee had done a good job, Jeremy thought. Jeremy had attended numerous of those get-togethers. He knew that they were necessary formalities, but the real work was to be done somewhere else. When preparing a rough outline of a business plan last night Jeremy had become aware of the monstrous undertaking he had gotten himself into. He needed to move very strategically, if he were not to disappoint Mzee.

Mzee was asked by the Chairman to introduce his ideas. Most persons present were aware what Mzee had in mind: an agricultural venture for high-value products, to be owned by the farmers, on a fully-serviced location. Mzee once more spelled it out and then introduced Jeremy: 'I'm an old man, but I still recognize the virtue of youth. I also know the value of ideas, but ideas without execution are useless. Youth can bring ideas to fruition. I'm happy to present to you Jeremy de

Besançon. I have known Jeremy for many years and he's my son's best friend. What's more important: Jeremy is a friend of Africa and has launched many successful projects on this continent. I have been witness to some of those, and to Jeremy's skills and commitment. Jeremy, would you like to say a few words?'

Jeremy knew that this was a crucial moment: if he would not get the buy-in of all concerned he could as well pack his bags. More importantly: he needed it today; bureaucratic procrastination would not fit his calendar.

He began: 'Thank you all for being here, and a special thanks to Mzee for having invited me to work with you on what could be a very exciting project. We all know that in this region jobs are hard to come by and that, whatever jobs are there, they are not well paid. Not enough for feeding our families, for sending our children to school, for having the medical care when needed. Personally, I'm convinced that the richness of our planet is sufficient to offer all of us a decent and honourable existence. What it takes to make that happen is organization and commitment. I am not a magician to create change from one day to another. But I believe that Mzee has a great idea.'

'Allow me to elaborate: for a society, for an economy to function one needs to produce what is in demand. Mzee talked about a particular variety of roses that can be grown in this climate around the Kilimanjaro. Yes, it is true: people in Europe and elsewhere are prepared to pay high prices for those flowers. But it would be risky to bet on one single variety. I propose to look at a diversified range, not only flowers but also high quality vegetables which can be delivered fresh to the great restaurants in Europe. The market is there and I have some idea what the customers are prepared to pay.'

'But shouldn't our starting point be somewhere else? Shouldn't it be what us and our families need for a descent livelihood? Many of us work long hours and yet have to take a second job to make ends meet. Wouldn't we want to change that if we had the chance? If we were to embark on this project I believe our starting point should be to ensure an income per family household of $500 per month.'

Jeremy paused for effect. He knew he had an audience now. Money speaks and the figure he had just mentioned amounted to several times the average monthly income in the country.

He continued: 'That's not all. In order to be successful our project needs to be totally self-sufficient in terms of water, electricity and social services. That's imperative from a commercial point of view, but also necessary for private households to function. And let's not be kidding, in order to be competitive on global markets we need first and foremost to be dependable suppliers at reasonable prices. One cannot at the same time be productive and stand in the queue with a sick child for medical care. Healthy workers for healthy profits: that's the first pillar of my proposal.'

'The second one is that of sustainability. Most of you remember the sisal story and many of you have been hurt. You don't want that to happen again. The land we intend to develop belongs to the State through the Moshi City Council. Mzee has obtained a freehold lease on the land and is prepared to sublet the estate for an indefinite period. There is no risk there: you all know Mzee. While the flower and vegetable growers will have to pay rent for their plots, they will be owners of their operations and be responsible for generating profits. How? In order to create economies of scale and to reduce marketing costs I propose that a company be created to take care of sales and logistics, fully owned by the growers as shareholders and overseen by an association in which all participants are equal members. One man, one vote. We will not be at the mercy of exploiting investors!'

Jeremy continued to provide further details of his ideas, at the same time encouraging questions. He talked about the need for technical expertise and training, management, quality control, trade financing, packaging and a range of other topics in which he had become an expert.

The convincing argument he had left for last: 'If the general principle appeals to you, a proper feasibility study will have to be carried out. If you so wish I can do that; I have some time on my hands and it would not cost you anything. If the outcome is positive, we will have to start a process of buy-in, from the Government and from the private sector. That partnership is crucial for success. After that, investments will have to be forthcoming, expertise to be obtained and an organizational structure to be put in place. I'm prepared to guarantee a loan from the Government, I'm also prepared to provide working capital for 18 months, to find first-class expertise and to be your management adviser for a period to be determined.'

Jeremy paused again. There was no reaction. He went on: 'You may ask why I'm doing this, making you this proposal. The answer is simple: Africa has given me much and I would like to give something back. There is only one condition, Mr Chairman, and that is this: today I would like to receive the green light from all of you that we go ahead.'

The Permanent Secretary was a bit puzzled: this was not how things were done normally. One would close a meeting with saying that it had been very useful and that one was looking forward to another one. This Jeremy guy wanted a decision, here and now. He looked at Mzee, who nodded, then looked at the Mayor, who looked at Mzee and then also nodded. 'Well, ladies and gentlemen', the Permanent Secretary then said, 'will all of you in favour of letting Jeremy do his feasibility study raise their hands.' All did, and Jeremy knew that with that gesture another door towards going back on the Sarah road had been closed.

Twenty

Jacques was already at the "Café du Théatre" when Sarah arrived. On her way, Sarah had once more asked herself why she had called him. Was it because she wanted to take revenge on Jeremy, choosing the Café as a venue, Jeremy's "dining room", for a date with a former lover? Would she want to see whether there was a way back to Jacques, a year after she had walked out on him?

There was maybe some truth in the first option, but she discarded the latter one right away: they had lived together for three years, but she had not felt any like-mindedness. That had led to competing on all sorts of issues, with little readiness to look for compromise. She had packed her bags and moved out. They had met a few times at social functions afterwards, but had not remained in regular contact. There was no desire to go back to Jacques. Why had she called him? She didn't know; she just had.

Fernando was at the door when Sarah entered. 'Good evening, Madam. Nice seeing you again. Will Jeremy be there as well? Shall I guide you to his table?' Oops, that hurts, Sarah thought. 'No, thank you, Fernando. Jeremy is on a business trip and I will be meeting an old friend for drinks.' 'Of course, Madam, and my greetings to Jeremy when you speak to him.'

Fat chance, Sarah thought and moved to the bar where she had spotted Jacques.

'Hello, beautiful', Jacques greeted her, 'what a surprise! What's up? But first, what would you like to drink? The usual? A Perrier?' 'Hello, Jacques. I would like a glass of white wine, please', Sarah replied and set down on the stool next to him. 'Well, things certainly have changed', Jacques reacted, rather surprised, and placed the order.

They exchanged a few updates on their professional lives over the last year and then Sarah began: 'Jacques, I don't know why I've called you, but there must be a reason, and thanks for coming. Let me tell you my story and when hearing myself talk, things may become clearer. I will not give you all the details, but feel free to ask questions.'

'During the last week or so I have been in situations that have made a profound impact on me. Both positive and negative. The negative side almost destroyed me emotionally. Yes, it has to do with a man, who came and went. I desperately want him back, but increasingly I'm aware that there might be a bigger picture. I'm looking for clues and I think that's why I called you.'

Jacques was pensive and looked rather serious. 'Are you seeing a professional?' he asked. 'Not yet', Sarah replied, 'I have an appointment on Monday with a counsellor. You know me well and maybe you can put me on the right footing before I enter his office.' 'Tall order', Jacques replied, 'but let me give it a try. The details of this man's arrival and departure I don't have. He will probably not come back. It hardly ever happens.' That was not what Sarah wished to hear and she almost regretted that she had asked for this rendezvous.

Jacques continued: 'I'm glad that you recognized that there might be a "bigger picture" and that you have decided to see a professional. I will not enter his domain. What I can do, now that some time has passed and that we have taken some distance from each other, is to give you my perspective on the evolution of our relationship.'

'Go ahead,' Sarah encouraged him. Jacques ordered another round of drinks and then continued: 'I used the word "evolution" because there was change. I said from *my* perspective, because I believe *you* changed. We could open a can of worms here, as we have done so often when we were still together. But you did not propose our get-together tonight to settle old scores or to start a new fight. So, you want me to go on?'

'Please do', Sarah said, being rather apprehensive of the imminent arrival of an unpleasant truth.

'When we were together, and after the initial euphoria had blown over, we could not, simply could not step outside and get the helicopter view of what was going on. That's different now and I'm telling you that I've spent many an hour on trying to figure out why we were incapable of making our relationship work. Of course, I was a 50 per cent stakeholder in our venture and assume my responsibilities as such. But that's not what you have come to discuss. You're looking for clues. Let me see whether I can help.'

'When we started to recognize that the honeymoon was over, we began to mark our territories and compete for supremacy. That is "normal" when the "us" gives way to "you and me". I became conscious of that and tried to give you space. Instead of becoming more comfortable you seemed to struggle with that additional space: a fight you could control, freedom you couldn't. You began to work longer hours, up to 12 hours per day, sometimes seven days per week. That was something you *could* control. Finally our relationship and I became irrelevant, even an irritating accessory to your life and you walked out. I'm sorry for being so direct, but that's how I see things. Does it make sense to you?'

Sarah did not react, pondering her thoughts. She had expected something else, something more "pedestrian", like the proverbial: "You never screwed the cap back on the toothpaste tube after brushing your teeth". Jacques' remarks were rather profound. Could it be that her dealings with life were so different from how she had experienced those? Very likely. Could it be that her inclination to wanting control "life" – which she recognized – had led to the opposite of the desired results? She would have to think about that.

'Jacques, thank you for what you just said. You probably have quite a few things to add, but I would prefer to leave it at that.' Sarah put her hand on his and looked him in the eyes: 'And if I have hurt you with my actions, I would like you to know that I'm terribly sorry.'

'Don't worry', Jacques replied, 'I may have been off the mark myself. That's all a thing of the past. What matters now is that you find your bearings. You have been suffering and you show that you don't want that. That is a starting point. Now the real work begins. I wish you all the best and I know that you will succeed.' He gave Sarah a little peck on her cheek and for the first time since almost 24 hours Sarah saw a glimmer of hope.

134

Twenty-one

Jeremy returned with Mzee to Arusha. He was excited. Kis, when he had phoned Jeremy a few weeks ago, had given him only a vague idea of what Mzee had in mind. Yesterday, Mzee had provided further detail. Last night Jeremy had started to sketch the outline of a plan and this morning he had been given the green light to go ahead. The real work could begin! He would stay one more day in Mzee's house and pick the old man's brains. Then he would install himself in Moshi, find a place to live, hire a car, buy a bike, create some kind of an office and take off. Yes, Jeremy was excited.

Although he had told "everybody" that he would be gone for an "indefinite" period of time, from the outset he had set himself a deadline. That was the way he worked; he simply couldn't function in an open-ended structure. Three months, he had given himself. In three months' time he would design the project in all its operational detail, he would get all stakeholders on board, the financing arranged, the organizational structures in place and then he would return to Europe.

What he had *not* told anybody, not even Mzee, was that he needed Kis to run the show after his departure. For such a huge undertaking to be successful there has to be a "champion", someone to inspire a team, someone who represents the glue to keep together hundreds of individual pieces. Kis could do that better than anybody else, but he needed to be convinced and that would not be easy, Jeremy knew. Anyway, that was not for now. Jeremy's first priority was to construct a firm business plan, formulate all questions, find all answers and then he would "attack" Kis. Jeremy knew himself well: he would not take "no" for an answer.

Yes, Jeremy was excited, but there was a shadow hanging over his euphoria and that shadow had a name: Sarah. Sarah continued to be on his mind and while he stuck to his believe that he had taken the right decision, her sufferings hurt him. I have to live with that, Jeremy knew, without giving any further reign to that lingering sense of discomfort.

Twenty-two

'May I call you Sarah?' Dr Lemaire asked after Sarah had taken a seat in his consulting room. Lemaire appeared to be a very charming man; young and lively, not at all the archetype of a shrink. Sarah felt right away comfortable with him. 'Please do', she responded, being grateful to Terry for having arranged this encounter. It had been a better day today. Her discussion with Jacques Friday night had been useful. 'Now the real work begins', he had said. Whatever that work would be, she did not know, but "work" she could deal with. That was her domain.

The weekend she had spent in her shop, pretending to work but not accomplishing very much. Coming home last night Sarah had again been confronted with the "scene of the crime", by traces of beer and milk on the wall, which she still had not cleaned up. Depression struck once more and she headed for the bar, looking for the bottle of Chivas: empty. Just as well, Sarah had thought, without knowing that Terry had been her guardian angel. She had poured herself a glass of white wine instead and set down on the couch. She had felt totally drained, almost emotionless and had gone to bed. She had slept 12 hours in one stretch.

Today she had felt much better, had been productive at work and now sitting in Lemaire's consulting room, there was a bit of a warm bath feeling: this man would take care of her. Here she was safe and together they would be working on getting her out of her misery and on getting Jeremy back.

'What seems to be the problem?' Lemaire encouraged her. 'I don't quite know', Sarah admitted honestly. 'Maybe you can help me figure it out. Let me start with what happened over the last two weeks and then I'll let you put the puzzle pieces together.'

Lemaire burst out into laughter, a warm, honest laugh. 'I see, you want to be in charge of this session, telling me what to do. That's fine with me; saves me a lot of effort. Are you always like that: wanting to be in control of things?'

Sarah was taken aback. That had not at all been her intention. She had come to Lemaire for help, to uncover the hidden corners of her character, to become a "whole" person, whatever that might be, and of course, to get Jeremy back.

'I'm sorry, doctor, that's not how I wanted it to sound, but you're right: I do have a tendency to wish to control things.' 'All right', Lemaire reacted, 'just joking. Please start wherever you would like to begin your story.'

Sarah began. Having told Terry the Jeremy story twice had helped her in putting a certain structure in her experiences of late. But with Lemaire she tried a different tack. "Doctor, what should I do to get the man I love back into my life?' Lemaire did not blink and said with a straight face: 'Nothing, absolutely nothing!' He did not say anything more. Sarah became uneasy. That was not what she wanted to hear and she did not seem to make much progress with Lemaire.

'OK, let me give you the story about this man. His name is Jeremy. I have not been dating for some time, as I was rather frustrated by past experiences. By the way, I'm 38 years of age, my father was British, my mother Swedish; they both passed away. Two weeks ago I met this Jeremy guy', and Sarah continued her story chapter by chapter, paragraph by paragraph, line by line, including her discussions with Terry and with Jacques. It took her half an hour to lay it all out, while Lemaire was taking notes from time to time.

'Quite a story', he finally said, 'but why have you come to *me*?' To get Jeremy back, Sarah thought, but did not say; Lemaire had already killed that option. Then she recalled her discussions with Jeremy – she had almost forgotten her discussions with him – , about her confusions of late, so much was her mind clouded-over by the recent events. She had explicitly asked Jeremy, when they first had dinner at her place, whether she should seek professional help. He had said "yes". She also, vaguely, remembered Terry's observation: 'You haven't been yourself off late. See somebody!' And it was Terry who had organized this rendezvous. People around her had seen something that Sarah had not noticed and had gently nudged her towards "counselling". But where should she begin when opening up to Lemaire? She gave it a shot: 'Jeremy thinks that I've arrived at some kind of crossroads in my life. If so, I would very much like to know where I'm coming from and where I'm heading.'

'Fine', Lemaire reacted, 'together we may be able to figure that out. But not today, it will take us a bit of work and time. This afternoon I have the following to say: the agony, the profound suffering which Jeremy's departure caused you is probably the result of something else that happened in your life. You and I will try to uncover that event or set of circumstances. Once you are conscious of what the "real" reason is you will be able to give the pain caused by Jeremy's departure its proper place and it will no longer be as devastating for you. A good starting point right now would be to try to convince yourself of that: it's not Jeremy, it's me. In fact, you might discover a certain gratefulness for what you consider Jeremy's cruelness. He triggered a crisis in your life, which subsequently gave you the impulse to look for the bigger cause.'

Sarah had to think about that: yes, her life had been full of "events" with delayed impact on her appreciation of things at a later date. But she could not see the link between those and Jeremy's departure. Jeremy – ever so briefly – had been her "mountain", the *solution* to her uncertainties, not the *cause*! It was his *presence* that gave her energy; it was his *absence* that deprived her of it. What was Lemaire saying?

'Thank you, doctor. I'm not sure that I fully understand the blessing of Jeremy's departure. But, of course, I would love to see it that way and be relieved of my pain. I very much want to work with you on unravelling myself and I look forward to our next session. In the meantime would you have a suggestion as to how to deal with the Jeremy dilemma? To tell you the truth: I'm ready to jump into a plane and search for him, all over Africa, even without being sure that he will be there!'

'If that doesn't make you feel uncomfortable, please call me Henri', Lemaire replied. 'Now, Jeremy: I've already suggested that Jeremy is not your struggle. It may take you some time to accept that. My advice to you is: avoid chasing him. He has not responded to your calls and e-mails and most likely will not do so in future. Waiting in front of your computer for a message from him devours precious energy. In addition, *if,* and that's a big if, Jeremy decides to come back to you, he will do so on his own free will. Not because you "ordered" him.

Right now, you will not be able to "forget" him and the pain will be there for some time, but if you manage to refocus your emotions towards discovering the "real" Sarah you will have embarked on a much more positive and powerful path to replenish your depleted energy reservoir.'

Lemaire opened his agenda and leafed through the pages. 'Same time, same place next week?' he suggested. Sarah got up and gave him a kiss on his cheek. 'Thank you, Henri, I look forward to that.'

Twenty-three

'Kis, my friend! How are you?' 'Hi stranger, what's up?' Kis and Jeremy did not need more than that to connect. Jeremy had felt that the time had come to play the Kis card, or at least to do some groundwork in that direction. "Groundwork" Jeremy had done to quite an extend on his flower project, since his arrival in Arusha, four weeks ago. He had found a house, outside Moshi with a view on the Kilimanjaro, had established an office in the centre of town, recruited staff and he was on the move. For most of the day he would be "in the field", often on his bike, checking the terrain and visualizing the eventual lay-out of nurseries, roads, buildings, irrigation channels and the physical infrastructure in general. In the late afternoon he would return to his office and sit down behind his computer, design a variety of scenarios and enter vast quantities of data. Jeremy enjoyed what he was doing, but most of all he got a kick out of working and living with the people of the region.

Over time Moshi had grown into a city of over 150,000 inhabitants, but in character it had very much remained a farmers' village. Jeremy loved to mingle with the "locals" and speaking their language made establishing social contacts ever so easy. The news of the possible creation of a huge flower farm had spread like wildfire and Jeremy's role in the venture was well known. Many people remembered him from his "Steinweg days"; now Jeremy had been become a "star". He did not like that; he preferred to develop this project in a low-key fashion, so as not to create expectations. Yet, having good contacts with the local community were essential for the project's success. It had given him the opportunity to spot potential key-players in its execution and gradually an enthusiastic team of would-be managers had started to form. Now the time had come to attack the marketing side of things and to align the supply and demand dynamics. It was time to call Kis.

Jeremy gave Kis an update on the state of affairs in Moshi and could sense a certain excitement, even envy, on the other end of the line. 'And how is London?' Jeremy asked. 'Well, I have been extremely busy with my consulting work. Business is streaming in, and in the absence of good staff, I have to do most of the nitty-gritty myself. Fortunately, last week I have been able to recruit a few top-notch guys who will take a load off my shoulders, but I'm telling you: I could do with a break!'

'Well', Jeremy reacted without missing a beat, 'in that case I have a proposition to make: fly over to Arusha and we will climb the Kilimanjaro once more.' Kis hesitated and then came around: 'Actually, that sounds rather tempting. I haven't seen my father for a while and the physical challenge of a climb would do my body a lot of good. Let me see whether and how I can organize my work and I'll call you back in a day or so.'

'Great!' Jeremy responded enthusiastically. 'Meanwhile I have to ask you a big favour. I haven't told you so, but before I left I met a woman. A terrific person and you know me, when I say something like that I'm bloody serious. She is a bit in a bind right now and I'll give you the details later. Before you come to Arusha I would like you to go and see her. I want to know how she is and whether she is making progress with her struggles. By no means should she find out that you and I know each other. I told her about Kis, so you should change your name. You might wish to pretend that you have decided to move to my city and that you need help in finding a house and in decorating it for you. Will you do that for me?'

'Wow!' Kis reacted, 'that sounds like fun. Of course, I'll do that for you. Give me all I need to know, or what you care to share.' It became a long conversation. Kis and Jeremy had been entangled, jointly or separately, in quite a few emotional adventures and had developed a fine understanding for each other's sentiments. Yet, this Sarah story was quite something and Jeremy took his time to give it to Kis in all its painstaking detail.

After the telephone call Jeremy felt relieved: yes, he was looking forward to seeing his friend – and eventually making him responsible for his project – but more importantly, through Kis Jeremy would re-establish contact with Sarah. He was very happy about that. Sarah had been on his mind, in spite of his busy schedule, almost every day. He had not gone back on his belief that he had made the right decision to leave her. Now he had said to Kis: 'I intuitively feel that Sarah is my destiny.' Had that always been there, that intuition? And what would that destiny be? Jeremy had trained himself very well over the years: there would always be many questions but precious few answers. He could live with that.

Twenty-four

'You're thirty-eight. Have you ever had the wish to have children?' Henri Lemaire asked when Sarah returned to his office a week later.

'I've thought about that, but, firstly, none of my partners I saw as the father of my children. Of course, I could raise children on my own, but I don't consider that fair to them. Secondly, I wouldn't like to make the same mistake as my mother did.'

'What do you remember about your mother and your childhood', Lemaire probed.

'To tell you the truth: I don't remember very much. I hardly ever saw my mother. She adored the cocktail circuit of which my parents were part. She was a beautiful woman and loved to dress up. I think that that was her life and that she considered me an unwelcome accessory to her daily occupations. I don't remember ever having felt being loved by her.'

Lemaire looked at Sarah without speaking. Sarah paused. She had told Jeremy that she had "detested" her mother, now she had told Lemaire that she had never felt being loved by her mother. Was that the same?

Lemaire guessed her thoughts: 'You know, Sarah, it's never too late to love or to be loved, even in the case of your mother who is deceased. I will come back to that as we advance. Meanwhile, you have given an important clue with respect to the agony you felt when Jeremy left. You relived the lack of love you felt when you were a toddler.'

Sarah had an "ah-ha" moment. Yes, she felt *victimized* by Jeremy. If Lemaire's analysis was correct, the ball would be in *her* court. *She* could work on removing that dark feeling. It was up to *her*, not *Jeremy* to right things. What a wonderful opening had Lemaire just given her.

'Henri, I love you!' Sarah exclaimed, being right away shocked at what she had just said. 'Oh, I'm sorry. I shouldn't have said that, but you've just given me a wonderful insight. I feel so much better!'

'I'm glad to hear that, but – not to dampen your enthusiasm – we're not there yet. Tell me about your father.'

Lemaire continued soul-searching and Sarah happily let him. During this session, and the next one and the next one, Henri Lemaire helped Sarah to peel the numerous layers of her conditioned ego and to bring her closer to the original "self".

Twenty-five

Sarah's life had retaken a sense of "normalcy", albeit with some significant differences. She spent less hours at work and often closed her shop altogether. 'Terry let's go to a show', she would say and take off with her. They also had lengthy lunches together; no dinners, though, as Terry insisted on giving her "family life" its deserved place.

They talked a lot, but the word "Jeremy" was out of bounds. Instead Sarah gave Terry glimpses of her discussions with Lemaire and at times asked for a second opinion. But most of the time they talked about "business", not so much "content", rather "form". "Content" was what Sarah was good at, it was "form" that disturbed her. While she continued to get a kick out of her creative work, her dealings with the likes of Mme de Fontebleu increasingly put her off. She had already put the brakes on a few lucrative assignments, but where would that lead to? There were bills to be paid!

She had put her confusion in front of Terry (Terry has become a real friend, Sarah had gratefully thought on a number of occasions). Terry had not said much more than: 'Look, in my view – and I know your calendar – there is a lot of scope for reducing your workload. How and why could be debated and obviously you'll be the one to decide. Why don't you ask Lemaire to help you in sorting that out?' 'Thanks, Terry', Sarah had replied, I'll take that route. Meanwhile I would like you to know how much I value our friendship. Without you I might have jumped off the cliff.' 'Maybe not', Terry had said, 'and it does me a lot of good to see that you're not likely to do so anytime soon!'

'Henri, how long is this going to take?' Sarah rather pointedly asked when they met next. 'How long is *what* going to take?' Lemaire reacted, with a chuckle. 'Let's say: my recovery and my discovery of the "self"?' Lemaire looked at Sarah and said: 'You tell *me*.'

'Henri, stop playing games with me. You're the doctor, I'm the patient. When I have the flu, a doctor can tell me that with proper care it may be gone in seven days. Your therapy: how long will it last before I find Nirvana?' 'Did I hear you say: "Before *I* find Nirvana?" Could it be possible that Nirvana – whatever that might represent – finds *you*, once you let it? That you still want to control the uncontrollable?'

Sarah was quiet; had she fallen in an old trap? 'Sorry, Henri, I went off the tracks. Please, talk to me.'

'OK, thanks. There is some legitimacy to your question. It's the first thing a physically ill person asks the doctor: when will I get better? But here we are talking about different phenomena. And they are much less exact or even scientific. Yet, there is a body of historical evidence that suggests a convergence of certain trains of thoughts. I will not take you to Freud or other great thinkers. Let's see whether I can find some plain language to explain.'

'*You* have decided to seek help and that's an enormous first step. The crisis you've experienced might have blown a few fuses in your neurological circuits, and that needs healing. Personally, I'm against prescribing medication for that. You're a strong woman, physically healthy and I believe your body will take care of that. The rest is a process of reflection, of gaining consciousness of what's happening with, inside and around you, of continuously questioning your motives, of spring-cleaning and of exploring new avenues. It will be an upward trajectory, but not a straight line. There will be moments of helplessness and despair when you find yourself in unchartered territory. But you'll find energy and courage in accepting those moods. If there is one word I would like you to adopt as your mantra it is: "surrender". That will not be easy for a strong-willed person like you, but it is possible. Life is much stronger than you are; why fight it?'

'Coming back to your question: "How long is this journey going to last?" One year, two, three? I can't tell. What I can tell is that it's a journey of diminishing anxiety and of incremental confidence. In a way, it is a "happy" journey, full of discoveries and spiritual adventures. I don't have to accompany you all the way, but I suggest that you call on me from time to time, just to check that you haven't taken up old habits. Does what I just said make sense to you?'

Sarah did not react right away, trying to digest Lemaire's words. 'Yes, I think it does, but I have to think about it. I have one immediate question and that concerns the organization of my work. There are things that I enjoy and there other things that I don't, but that I feel I *have* to do. How do I go about that?'

'I believe you already have the answer, by asking the question', Lemaire reacted. 'Would you be good at doing things you don't like to do? Would the real Sarah be in harmony with things she detests? Let your heart lead the way and the outcome, in whatever form or shape will be beautiful.'

'Thank you, Henri, that is helpful. I would like to suggest that we take a break of our sessions and that I call you some time in future.' Henri laughed, his signature laugh: warm and honest: 'Still in charge, I see.'

He stood up and extended his hand to Sarah. 'Come back whenever you feel like it. It's a great pleasure working with you.'

Sarah returned to her shop where Terry was still busying away. Sarah pulled up a chair next to Terry's and took her hand. 'I don't know what to say, Terry, and I don't know how to thank you for all the support you've given me all those years and, more in particular, the last few months. I want you to know that I will be forever grateful to you. I've just been with Lemaire and he has helped me uncover some hidden truths and to move forward. Please cancel the Fontebleu assignment. No, in fact I will call the lady myself, tomorrow morning. I will not see Lemaire for some time to come. If I can ask you for one more favour it is simply to stay by my side when I flounder. Like right now, when I tell you that I miss Jeremy terribly.' Sarah put her arms around Terry and cried softly. But this time her tears signified honest gratitude.

Twenty-six

'Sarah, there is call for you', Terry shouted from behind her desk. 'Can you please take a message,' Sarah replied, while trying to concentrate on her design work. 'It's a gentleman who insists on speaking to you in person.' 'All right, I'll take him', and Sarah lifted the receiver from the phone: 'Sarah Appleton.'

'Good morning, Madam', Kis said. 'My name is Anthony Leiser and I'm calling you from London. Your name has been given to me by a good friend, who prefers to remain anonymous. I intend to open an office for my company in your city and am looking for a place to live there part of the year. I'm not thinking of just a pied-à-terre, no, something more classy. My work implies a lot of entertaining. I need space and glamour. You see what I mean?'

Oh no, not one of those snobs again, Sarah thought, and haven't I decided to cut those out of my portfolio of clients? 'Look, Mr Leiser, it's very nice to think of me, but I'm really snowed under with work right now. I don't think that I can take on another project.'

'I understand', Anthony replied, 'but my move will not be soon. It so happens that I will be in your neighbourhood tomorrow and if you could spare a few minutes I could explain to you what I have in mind and then you may decide whether my ideas appeal to you and on what terms we could work together.' Sarah hesitated: this man is rather insisting and she didn't like that. Yet, she was intrigued by the calm tone of his voice and she admitted a certain curiosity. 'OK, I could make some time tomorrow. Three o'clock in my shop?' 'Thank you, Madam. If it suits you, I know a little bistro not too far from where you work. It's called "Café du Théatre". I would be privileged if I could invite you for a cup of tea there.'

This man has done his homework, Sarah thought and her curiosity moved up a notch. She had not been back to the Café since her drinks with Jacques and the moments spent there with Jeremy remained a warm souvenir. She would agree. 'All right, see you there, Mr Leiser. Tomorrow at three.'

Twenty-seven

Jeremy was making good progress. The figures seemed to add up and, although he still needed the results of some soil samples and other tests, he was confident that he could come up with a credible proposal. Jeremy was looking forward to Kis' arrival. He was his best friend and the prospect of climbing the Kilimanjaro together was very exciting. Having to convince Kis to become involved in the project still remained a challenge, but he would take care of that when the moment was right.

Jeremy was sitting in front of his computer when Tira, his newly recruited secretary, walked in: 'Jeremy, there is a woman who would like to see you. She didn't want to give her name; she only said that you know her.' 'Bring her in', Jeremy said without looking up from the computer screen.

'Hi, Jeremy.' Jeremy recognized her voice and goose bumps crept up his spine. He raised his head: 'Lula, what the hell are you doing here?' 'Aren't you happy to see me?' Lula asked when moving towards Jeremy, and gave him a kiss. 'Yes, of course I am, but I was not expecting you. How did you find me?' 'I will tell you, but aren't you offering me a drink?' 'OK, let me finish this business, close my computer and we'll have a drink. Just two minutes. Please grab something to read.'

While Jeremy went about saving his data, thoughts were racing through his head: what was the significance of Lula's appearance? What did she want? After their brief marriage ten years ago, they had never met again. Now that he was quietly making progress with his project and appeared to be on top of things, he definitely did not need a troublemaker, someone who would try to pull the rug from under him.

He had met Lula in Kampala, the capital of Uganda. She was the Personal Assistant of a Minister he had done business with and befriended. Lula was – and still is, Jeremy had noticed – a beautiful woman: tall, fine features and a radiant ebony skin. She had told him that she was a princess, hailing from the Baganda tribe, although Jeremy had never cared to find out whether that was true. From one thing came another and they had become a couple. When Jeremy had finished his business in Uganda and time had come to leave for another African destiny Lula had insisted on coming along and – simply – not to complicate his movements Jeremy had agreed to marry her. But the romance faded quickly. Lula had turned out to be a demanding woman, insisting on her royal pedigree and on being treated as such. She did not understand why Jeremy was so preoccupied with improving the lot of the poor. The poor were born that way, were they not? And wasn't she royalty? Jeremy had become conscious that Lula was an obstacle in accomplishing his mission and had asked for a divorce. She had agreed, but only on the condition that a considerable sum of money would come her way. And now: here she was again. It made Jeremy nervous. What could she be up to?

'OK, I'm ready. Let's go', Jeremy said and: 'Tira, can you please lock-up? See you tomorrow.' He took Lula by the arm and let her out of the office. There was a beer garden not far away, where they sat down and ordered drinks.

'So nice to see you, Jeremy', Lula said when lifting her glass to a toast, 'you're as handsome as ever. Certainly by now some beauty has ensnared you?' 'Not really', Jeremy responded, almost as in defence, 'but how did you know I was in Moshi?' 'That's not too difficult', Lula replied. 'You know how the jungle drums work. I'm back in Uganda and have been invited to occupy a position of a certain power. I think I'm good at what at what I'm doing and that's partly thanks to being well-informed. One of my sources told me about your latest "do-good" project. You know, we grow roses in Uganda as well. I thought that you and I might learn a thing or two from each other.'

Lula laid her hand on Jeremy's arm and gave him a mischievous wink. Jeremy was not at all comfortable with the situation and decided to steer the conversation in a different direction.

'Lula, you must know that I'm very pleased to see you after so many years. Forget about the roses, the project I mean. Now that you're here I would like to ask of you something else. Our marriage was not what one would call a success, but that's the past. I don't believe in revisiting the past, with only one exception and that is to learn from it. Ten years have passed and that has given us a valuable window of perspective. Is there anything that you would like to tell me now that you haven't conveyed then?'

Lula looked at Jeremy, gave him a warm smile, put her arms around his shoulders and said: 'Jeremy, don't be so serious. Let's have some fun!' 'No', Jeremy reacted, 'I *am* serious!' Lula could see that and she backed off.

'Honestly, Jeremy, is there a woman in your life?' Lula tried. 'No, not right now, but there might be', Jeremy replied rather enigmatically, 'and I don't want to make mistakes. Tell me, in retrospect, how do you see me?'

Lula was silent for a moment, obviously reflecting on what to say. She had come to spy on what Jeremy was concocting in Moshi. She would get him drunk, seduce him and in the process extract valuable information from him. But Jeremy didn't bite, at least not yet. All right, let's play his game first and then it will be my turn, Lula thought and began to speak.

'You know that I have an enormous admiration for you as a person and for what you do. You have a big heart, full of compassion and a single-minded drive to turn your emotions into action. I think that is what attracted me most in you. Of course, the fact that you're stunningly handsome also helped!'

She winked again, but Jeremy did not react. 'Describing *you* is one thing, analysing our relationship and why it failed is something else. Obviously, you wanted me to say something about the latter. In your single-mindedness you often think of yourself as the omnipotent centre of the universe. Sorry, that sounds rather heavy, but I say it to make a point. There may be views that you don't share, but nevertheless have value, at least for others. You and I had different views. I did not perceive any effort on your part to accommodate mine, rather an obsessive insistence to impose yours. Should I say more?'

'No, that will do', Jeremy replied rather sombrely. Lula had told him something that he would have to reflect on, but later. One message he registered right away: what one person might consider a positive character trait, another might interpret as a formidable weakness. 'Thank you for what you just said. I will give it serious thought. Now it is my turn to tell you why I'm here and what I'm doing.'

Jeremy knew his little Lula and had no intention to give her more than absolutely necessary. He had done his homework and knew that there was some flower growing business going on in Uganda, as in many other parts of the world. It was not his intention to start competition; his game plan was to find the niches in global demand. But he would not share his ideas with others, certainly not with Lula. First, he gave her an update on some of latest adventures, just anecdotal stuff. Then he asked Lula for her stories (nothing has changed, he thought when listening to her bragging, only with half an ear) and finally he touched on his project: He was *studying* options and possibilities, nothing more. It would be up to the local community to *decide*.

They had a few more beers and their conversation reached a lighter level of engagement. Lula touched Jeremy's arms or legs as if to make a point and winked at every opportunity. Jeremy couldn't help but admitting that he enjoyed being in Lula's company. Was it her, was it the alcohol? He didn't probe. 'Jeremy, shall we have something to eat? I'm staying at the "Aishi Machame" and they have a good kitchen.' 'Fine with me. After all, if one meets once every ten years one could as well make the most of it.'

On the backseat of the taxi taking them to the hotel Lula crawled into Jeremy's torso as if they were first-time lovers. Giggling, arms hooked, they entered the restaurant. Lula was known here, Jeremy observed, as she was right away shown her table. 'Two waragi's, please', she ordered, even before they had sat down. Help, Jeremy prayed, knowing this potent Ugandan banana liquor, let me not go under.

They had their meal, a few bottles of wine to go with it and over coffee Lula leaned over to Jeremy, drunk or pretending to be drunk – Jeremy couldn't say – and whispered: 'Darling, what I haven't told you when you asked me this afternoon how I see you, is that I think of you as a terrific lover. In fact, you're by far the best lover I've ever had. You play my body as if it were a piano. Please come to my room and take me to heaven.'

The word piano had a sobering effect on Jeremy, as a cold shower. Not that he had had the intention to giving in to Lula's advances, but the word piano made him think of the Steinweg and Sarah. He wanted to stay the course. He took Lula in his arms – that was not difficult as she was already stretched out over his lap – stroked her hair and simply said: 'Lula, you're beautiful, but let's not.'

He asked for the bill, paid, took Lula to her room door, kissed her on her cheek, ordered a taxi at the reception and let himself be driven home. Wanting to always be in charge might not be a good character trait, he thought while reflecting on the events of the day, but tonight I have avoided a lot of trouble by insisting on staying on top – and that not in the sexual sense.

Twenty-eight

Sarah had not asked Mr Leiser how she would recognize him. She looked around at the Café to spot a single person sitting at a table, but apart from an African, reading a newspaper, there were only couples or groups of people enjoying a mid-afternoon break. Fernando saw her, being a bit lost, and approached her. 'Good afternoon, Madam. What a pleasure seeing you. Are we awaiting Jeremy?' 'Hello, Fernando. No, Jeremy is still away on business. I have an appointment with a certain Mr Leiser. Would you happen to know him?'

Kis had been to the Café with Jeremy several times and on purpose he had arrived early today. 'Fernando', he had said after they had greeted each other as old buddies, 'I'm here to meet a friend of Jeremy's, but she should not know that Jeremy and I know each other. I'll explain some other time. Today my name is not Kis, but Anthony Leiser.'

Fernando had seen a lot of strange things in his life, and did not ask questions. Discretion was the name of the game in his profession. 'Of course, Mr Leiser. What can I get you to drink?' 'A Campari soda, please. And thank you, Fernando.'

'Please follow me', Fernando said and he headed for the table where the African was reading the Financial Times. 'Mr

Leiser, sorry to disturb you, but you have a visitor.' Kis put his newspaper down and stood up. 'Ms Appleton, I presume?' he said while offering her a bright smile and his hand. 'So nice of you to make time for me. Please, do sit down', and he pulled a chair out, while Fernando took Sarah's coat. 'What would you like to eat or drink?' Anthony asked Sarah. 'Nothing to eat, thank you. A mint tea, please.'

Anthony looked at Fernando, who, with a nod, acknowledged the order and left. What a handsome man, Sarah thought, tall, slim, athletic and very well dressed, but how come I thought I had a Caucasian on the line yesterday, not an African? I have travelled the world and I have learned to appreciate different cultures and I have a fine "nose" for ethnic differences. Never mind, let's see what Mr Leiser has to say.

Kis looked at Sarah. Jeremy had not exaggerated: this was quite a woman! Yes, she was pretty and elegant with her long blond hair and cobalt blue eyes. But that was not what struck him. She radiated inner beauty. There was calm, confidence and gentleness, but also, Kis thought, a certain fragility and vulnerability. 'May I give you my card?' Anthony said and handed Sarah an embossed piece of carton. Anthony Leiser was all it said. No title, address, telephone number or Web coordinates. How discrete, Sarah thought. 'Ms Appleton, once more, many thanks for seeing me at such short notice. Please call me Anthony.'

Fernando arrived with the mint tea and without saying a word put it in front of Sarah. 'You may call me Sarah', Sarah said and gave Kis her card. Kis looked at her once more, as if surveying a painting. He now fully understood why Jeremy had asked him for a favour and he would do his level best not to disappoint him.

'Sarah, I will tell you in a moment what I have in mind, but before doing so I'll tell you why I have approached *you*. I've heard about your work and about the *way* you work. That appealed to me and, being a bit choosy and knowing what I want, I decided: Sarah Appleton is the one who is going to my project.'

Anthony went on to explain his business, how he had started to build a network among high-flyers to sell art of unique value. How he had moved into the marketing of luxury goods and finally, how he had become a "guru" – he did not use that word; it was Sarah's interpretation – in international marketing, in general. He had established offices in various economic centres of the world and only the sky was the limit. Now he wanted to set up a place in Sarah's city and was looking for someone to help in finding and decorating an apartment.

'But, I lied to you', Anthony said rather abruptly, locking his eyes into Sarah's, 'when I said that I wanted a glamorous place to entertain my business friends. What I want is a place where *I* feel at home. Where there is harmony between who I am and my surroundings. In fact, *that*'s why I called you.'

Sarah did not react; there were thoughts in her head that needed to be addressed. When Anthony talked to her she had instantly felt a rapport with this man. He appeared sincere. But why had he just said that he had lied to her? Why lying and why admitting it? She would throw out a teaser: 'Anthony, once more, thanks for thinking that I may be useful and for sharing some of your stories with me. Let me give a bit of my own background and philosophy.' 'With the greatest pleasure,' Anthony interjected, 'but before you do so: would you care for something else to drink?'

Sarah looked at her watch; she had no other engagements that afternoon. 'A glass of Chardonnay would be fine,' she replied. Anthony waved at Fernando without calling his name. Fernando appeared: 'A Chardonnay for the lady, please and a Chivas for me. No ice.' 'Coming up', Fernando said, looking at Kis but not giving away the slightest sign of being an accomplice.

Sarah continued: 'Anthony, we don't know each other and we'll certainly have a lot more to discuss before I accept to work with you. But one thing you need to know. Yes, I have a reputation for delivering glamorous interiors for the rich and famous. But off late I have decided to stop doing that. My values in life – I'm beginning to discover – are real and not fake, and from now on I only work for people with whom I share at least some of those values.'

She looked Anthony in the eyes. He looked at hers and there was an understanding connection. The drinks were delivered and then it was Anthony's turn: 'Remarkable that you say that. I have become, what I could call in all modesty, rather successful in my business, because of my values and because of the people I chose to work with. But my question to you is: have you always been that way?'

Sarah hesitated. They were not discussing an interior decoration project; they were exchanging details about personal lives. What was she telling this stranger? Why was she giving him all that personal stuff? Would she have done that to a prospective client in the past? Was it Jeremy, her sessions with Henri, that had removed layers of fear and made her feel comfortable with baring her soul?

She took a deep breath, and without reflecting said: 'My father was a diplomat. A man I admired enormously. He was strong and straight as an iron rod. He shaped me. He made me stand for my opinions, whatever they were and I'm still following his example. Thanks to him I've become the successful businesswoman that people say I am today. I'm 38 and I've already made a career other people, much older, are jealous of. But, and that's a big but, some time ago – I don't know: a year, two years? – I felt that I was on a wrong path, or at least not on *my* path. I began to see illusion around me, something that wasn't *me*. It wasn't clear to me at the time; it's easy to find comfort in one's success and to aspire more of the same. And then something broke – I still don't know why I'm telling you all this – , a few weeks ago. With the help of a professional I'm trying to restructure my life, to be in touch with the "real" me, who in turn can reach out to the "real" others. I still love my work and I am grateful for the talents given to me, but I will interact differently with the world around me.' There were tears coming out of Sarah's eyes, which she wiped away quickly.

There was no need for Kis to react: all had been said. Sarah broke the silence: 'By the way, where do you come from?' 'Tanzania', Anthony replied, 'I was born there.' 'Where in Tanzania?' Sarah wanted to know. 'Arusha', Anthony said, wondering whether he was giving away too much. 'Arusha!' Sarah exclaimed. 'I have a friend who spent time there. He once found a piano in Arusha, a real Steinweg and it changed his life. I lost contact with him and I miss him dearly. He had a friend in Arusha, called Kis. Does that name ring a bell?'

'No, it doesn't', Anthony said and felt that the time had come to leave: he had done his job and, although tempted, did not want to say: 'Jeremy misses you too.' He got up: 'Sarah, it was great meeting you. I'm leaving on a rather long business trip. Once I'm back, I'll give you a call and I'm sure we can work together.' 'Say "hi" to Arusha, in case your business trip might take you there', Sarah said, thinking of Jeremy. 'I will', Kis replied, also thinking of Jeremy.

174

Twenty-nine

Kis took a taxi to the airport and a plane back to London. Sarah stayed behind in the Café and ordered another glass of Chardonnay. She wanted a little time to digest her encounter with Anthony. Why had she told him about her father and the current discomfort with her business? Why had she given him personal details that she normally would not share with anybody? Was it the quiet confidence Anthony had radiated, that made her feel comfortable to open up? Or was it that the sessions with Lemaire were having an effect on her?

During a recent visit to his office Lemaire had wanted to come back to her relationship with her parents. 'What may have happened', Lemaire had volunteered, 'is that the lack of love you felt from your mother's side, drove you towards your father, and that in an exaggerated way you approved of everything he stood for. You recognized his values as "absolute" and adopted those as your own. But, what would be right for him might not have been right for you, although you might have adopted your father's dogmas as unshakeable truths. What often happens in one's life, at some point in time, is that the true "self" wants to shake that unnatural straightjacket. And that hurts, and manifests itself as a "crisis". The "modern" man and woman are not quite equipped for that, and feel lost. Maybe you're going through that process. Let's find out.'

'What I propose we do are two things: first, finding a way for you to recognize what's true and false. Together we might be able to identify rubbish and push it overboard. What's next is a bit more delicate: giving space to that beautiful creature that you are! The result of that will be a different Sarah, not necessarily a better Sarah, but at least a Sarah who can live in harmony with herself.'

Sarah had liked what Lemaire had told her and had wholeheartedly committed herself to continue working with him. Had that exchange with Lemaire contributed to fearlessly trust Anthony and tell him about her father, about the discomfort with certain aspects of her work and about Jeremy?

The wine began to have its effect on Sarah and Jeremy reappeared in her thoughts. It was over a month since he had left, but *how much* did she still miss him. Should she send him an SMS and tell him so? Lemaire had said: 'Do nothing, absolutely nothing!' But if sending Jeremy a message would make her feel good, was there any harm in that? She hesitated, then pulled out her mobile phone and composed an SMS: 'Just met a man from Arusha. I had to think of you.

Hope you're well, wherever you are. Love, Sarah.' She pushed the "send" button.

Sarah knew that she had sinned against Lemaire's instructions, but what the hell: it made her feel good. Sarah asked for the bill, paid and left. 'Give him my best when you talk to Jeremy', Fernando said at the door. 'I will', Sarah responded truthfully and ever so much wished that the opportunity would present itself.

Thirty

Jeremy had established a "Steering Committee", both to help him, and – primarily - to ensure the eventual adoption of his project. He had carefully selected its members: people who were in a position to press the "go" buttons, both in Government and in the private sector. Jeremy knew how important "sense of ownership" is for the success of a venture, like he was working on, and that the required enthusiasm needed to be carefully nurtured.

In the undertaking of his numerous projects Jeremy had learned an important thing: bribery would always backfire, generating self-interest was a much more effective option. The Steering Committee had met a couple of times and Jeremy had been successful on two scores: he been able to convince its members that they were engaged in a win-win proposition, and – Jeremy believed – he had been able to remove lingering doubts that this white Bwana – Jeremy – was out there to, once more, screw them over.

The Steering Committee had become a group of friends; yes, they battled over bolts and nuts and, of course, self- interests, but all of that in the good spirit of making progress. Their after-hours beer drinking sessions were a solid confirmation of having embarked on a joint adventure. Today's meeting was about to come to an end when Jeremy's mobile phone alerted him to a message. He didn't take it right away. Instead he said: 'Ladies and gentlemen, we have made a lot of progress. We will do our homework and meet two weeks from now, same place, same time. And before then: see you at the bar. Excuse me a moment while I have to take a call.'

Jeremy looked at his watch. It was five o'clock in Moshi, four o'clock in most parts of Europe. He opened his message box: Sarah. Jeremy was shaken, but quickly composed himself. After he read her message he was at the same time frustrated that he could not respond and relieved to know that Kis had been able to contact her.

He called Kis right away: 'Hey man, what's the scoop?' 'I'm not telling you', Kis teased him. 'That will have to wait until we meet, but I *can* say that I'm impressed: what a woman, this Sarah of yours!' 'Come on, tell me', Jeremy insisted. 'No, not now and don't you worry: Sarah is fine; she is receiving help and making good progress.'

'Listen, I've made my arrangements. I will fly out to Arusha coming Saturday and will be staying for two weeks. I leave it to you to organize our Kilimanjaro climb.' 'Terrific', Jeremy responded enthusiastically, being equally excited about the good news of Sarah and the forthcoming visit of Kis. Kis would fly out on Saturday and arrive on Sunday and that was only four days from now and some work had to be done to keep the project going while he would be gone. Jeremy didn't worry: he had been in similar situations before and he would also cope this time. 'Send me your flight details and I'll be at the airport. I will also inform Mzee. I look forward to seeing you, man!' Jeremy said and called off.

After Kis had tentatively agreed to come to Arusha, Jeremy had started preparations for climbing the Kilimanjaro, or Kili, as the mountain is affectionately known. It was now the beginning of June; a good month to climb old Kili. Chances of rain would be minimal, but the weather is always unpredictable around this "mother mountain". The last time Kis and Jeremy had been up – was it already 20 years ago? – they had taken the Machama Route. Jeremy recalled that it was also known as the Whiskey Route, but he had forgotten why. It had taken them about eight days, coming and going. For this occasion Jeremy had decided – and now obtained Kis' blessing – on a different trail: the Rongai Route for going up and the Muranga Route for coming down. He had done so on purpose: it would take them through some of the areas where Jeremy proposed to create the flower farms. When Jeremy's sources had warned that Rongai would be more dangerous than the more popular tourist trails, Jeremy had considered that an added incentive. But most importantly: the trip could be done in fewer days. Jeremy and Kis would be plenty busy and the flower project was priority # 1. Frolicking on Kili was one thing, but he needed Kis to have time to look at all nooks and crannies of his - until now, unknown to him – future. Jeremy's entire business plan had been designed in anticipation of Kis being the executor. Jeremy had taken a risk and he had no fallback position in case Kis would decline, other than taking the job himself. That was not an option: Jeremy needed to return to Europe!

Through his contacts in Moshi, Jeremy had provisionally arranged for a guide and four porters. He did not want to be part of an organized group: this was to be a Kis and Jeremy affair. He also wanted to avoid "established" huts, where they would have to mingle with people. Jeremy wanted to do the climb his way, with tents and supplies and for that choice of freedom he needed porters. After his brief talk with Kis, he placed a few calls and gave the "go" sign. Then he joined the Steering Committee, which was in a spirited session around a spectacular number of Kilimanjaro Lager bottles. Jeremy ordered another round: 'Cheers, my friends. Sorry for letting you wait, but I have good news for you. I just had Kis on the line and he will join us at our next meeting. 'To Kis', the Committee responded in unison and raised their glasses. They all (or almost all) knew Kis: the prodigal son of Mzee and were looking forward to his return. Another hurdle taken, Jeremy thought, and he joined the Committee in its cheerfulness.

Thirty-one

Saturday afternoon Jeremy travelled to Arusha. He had phoned Mzee to tell him that Kis was coming and Mzee was clearly excited. "How is the project coming along?' he had wanted to know. 'I'll tell you all about it before Kis arrives', Jeremy had said and had invited himself to Mzee's house, the day before Kis' arrival.

They were sitting on the veranda, enjoying a drink of whiskey. Jeremy had not seen Mzee since he had moved to Moshi, neither had he talked to him over the phone, until two days ago that is. It had been intentional on Jeremy's part. He had wanted to cover a whole lot of ground and *then* invite Mzee's inputs. Today was the day. He told Mzee all he had done and still intended to do, the challenges he had met and the solutions he considered appropriate, his engagement with people he found useful and his disregard of those he did not, the options for the way forward and the potential pitfalls to be avoided.

Mzee listened very carefully; he understood most of what Jeremy was telling him and what he didn't grasp right away he could well imagine. He knew Jeremy and his way of working. Yet, he had a feeling that Jeremy was hiding something.

Mzee poured Jeremy another whiskey and also offered himself a drop. Jeremy knew that that was the sign that Mzee wanted to speak, and became quiet.

'Jeremy, I'm proud of you and you have not disappointed me. As you can imagine, I've received a bit of feedback from my sources and I would like you to know that you have managed to generate quite a momentum for what you're trying to accomplish. Congratulations! By the way, you did well in sending that Lula of yours back to Uganda.'

Mzee chuckled and Jeremy felt slightly embarrassed. Mzee went on: 'For as much as I understand this business, what you've just told me makes sense to me. I also think that you've taken the right route with the Steering Committee. Later, I will have a few suggestions as to how best deal with some of its members, but before that, let me ask you something: How long will you stay?'

Jeremy was not prepared for that question; he had told everyone that his commitment would be indefinite, or sort of. For himself, it had been three months, at the most. Why was Mzee probing into that issue? Jeremy knew Mzee well: the man could look straight through you. There was no way of hiding.

Jeremy decided to play his cards open: 'Mzee, you're right. This project needs, literally and figuratively, a lot of nurturing, for years to come. Yes, I can come over from time to time, but certainly not be responsible for the running of this venture on a day to day basis.'

Jeremy stopped and helped himself to another shot of whiskey. Mzee declined when Jeremy offered. 'There is something I haven't told anybody, apart from Kis. Off late I have felt a pull towards the destiny of my life. You will guess: it is a woman. I cannot give you the details, at least not now, but it's her existence that now determines my decisions and actions, and that includes the Moshi project. Of course, I'm aware of the consequences and I've made a plan. It was not my intention to share it with you today, but since we're talking: I will. My only request to you is that the conversation remains between you and me. Agreed?'

'Agreed', Mzee replied and Jeremy knew that he could count on that promise. He began to elaborate in detail on his business plan, the various scenarios to ensure the promised income for the growers, the intricate linkages between supply and demand conditions, the projected growth – short and long term – to ensure the viability of the undertaking and a whole series of other topics.

Mzee listened, but did not know where Jeremy was heading. It would come, he figured, and it came. 'There is only one guy I know, who's capable of putting that together', Jeremy finally said, 'and that is Kis. I have invited him to come over to climb Kili. But the real reason is to convince him that he's the best man for the job.'

Mzee set back and looked at Mount Meru in the distance and at the setting sun – or the setting earth, as he preferred to call it - and there was a little smile on his face. He took his glass and emptied it. 'Well done, my son', he said finally, 'I'll leave it to the two of you to work it out.'

Thirty-two

Kili was covered by a blanket of clouds; that's to say the Uhuru Peak was. Jeremy and Kis had been going for four days and the porters were making camp. At midnight they would break up for the final stretch. Afterwards they would immediately start their descent and, barring unforeseen circumstances, reach Marangu towards the end of the day, where a car would be waiting.

Clouds or no clouds, the duo did not care. They had had their vistas all along, for miles and miles, both over the Tanzanian and Kenyan plains. It had not all been pristine beauty: human fingerprints were all over the place. When driving from Moshi to Loitokitok, the trail's starting point, Kis had remarked: 'When I was a kid this was all forest and bushland. Look at it now: squatters all over the place, erosion everywhere and not a blade of grass for the cows to eat.'

It had been the subject of long discussions between the two friends, while they were finding their way up the mountain and during rest stops. Yes, both had agreed on a number of causes. But not on the remedies. They were fully aware that life expectancy in Africa had risen spectacularly over the last century – although AIDS had knocked the numbers down in more recent times – and that the population growth was among the highest in the world. Pressure on arable land was enormous and so was human impact on its environment. Jeremy and Kis had also agreed on the complex interaction of "modern" and "traditional" life, of "nature" and "technology".

But where it came to finding solutions, Jeremy and Kis had often disagreed. Kis had left Africa and had immersed himself in Western business life. Yes, he had retained certain traditional values, as he had conveyed to Sarah at their Café meeting, but the continent of his birth had become marginalized. On the business charts that he consulted daily Africa was not even a blip, leaving alone a bar. Speed and volume had become his points of reference and Africa didn't have much of either.

Jeremy had taken a different point of view: speed and volume will lead to the earth's destruction; preservation in a sustainable way will provide a future for our children. The fact that neither Jeremy nor Kis had children didn't seem to matter in their argument, but Jeremy reminded Kis of an old expression in Swahili: "We don't own the land. We're only guardians of it for the next generation." 'And, by the way', Jeremy had said, 'the fact that a luxury brand that you represent copy that slogan I find rather repulsive. Shape up, man!'

Apart from those playful debates, they had been enjoying their company together enormously. Jeremy had been at the airport to greet Kis on Sunday morning and from that moment on there had been that old sense of bonding. They had spent gratifying moments with Mzee during the day and in the evening Jeremy and Kis had reconnected with the watering holes, and their occupants, in town. Jeremy had been invited to join, on the piano, the band at Stiggy's. They had a blast, but until then they had not talked about Sarah, neither about the flower project. Apparently they had both felt that enjoying the moment should not be compromised.

Monday morning, with a slight hangover, they had left for Moshi and began to talk. Kis had begun, giving Jeremy his latest business exploits, albeit in a modest way. Jeremy had listened carefully, searching for hooks that would help him to nail Kis to the flower project, which he would bring up later.

First and foremost he had been interested in Sarah: 'Tell me all, as you promised.' Kis had given him a full account of his visit. Line by line. His telephone call, Sarah's initial refusal to see him, his name change to Anthony Leiser (and how his secretary had manufactured a few copies of his new business card on the office printer), his instructions to Fernando, their encounter at the Café, Sarah's admissions of discontent with some of her work, the story about her father's role model and that she had a friend who had spent time in Arusha, where he

189

had found a Steinweg piano, which had changed his life and whom she missed dearly.

'Those are the facts', Jeremy had responded, 'now your interpretation, please.' Kis had given it to him: 'I think that Sarah is a woman who insists on getting what she wants, but right now she might not know what it is. She seems to be aware of her confusion and she does her level best to find answers. She told me that she is seeing someone to help her with that. I'm not a specialist and have no idea how long that would take, but I'm impressed by her commitment. I don't know what you can do with my report, but I'm thankful to you that you thought I could be helpful.'

'Thank you, my friend', Jeremy had replied, 'you have been helpful indeed.'

Now, seated just below the Uhuru Peak, Jeremy had felt that the moment had come to start his "attack". The porters had set up the tents, a fire had been lit, dinner had been served and a bottle of Chivas had auspiciously appeared in front of the two men. It had been a beautiful night; the moving clouds over the crater, in the distance, were engaged in a majestic dance with the trillions of stars shining on the campsite. Apart from the sound of the crackling fire, there was nothing to be heard.

'Kis, once more, thank you for having visited Sarah. You know me and my family story. How my mother has had a great influence on me, and by the way: I still have to work that out. Since we met in London, you and I have had very few secrets for each other and we've closely followed each other's moves. Maybe I haven't told you everything about Sarah, or, rather what impact our encounter has had on me. But that's for later. Let me first tell you something on what I think could be a wonderful and life-changing proposition for the people of Moshi.'

Jeremy had laid it all out, first in technical details, knowing that that would stimulate Kis' interest. He had talked about the macro picture: the profitability projections and the expected returns on investment. Then Jeremy had moved on to the micro levels: the impact on the livelihood of the people, the potential of improving the quality of their lives and the importance of giving them a handle on their destiny. He had tried to pass on to Kis the excitement he had felt when introducing the project to the Moshi people, how the notion of ownership had galvanized them.

Jeremy had sensed that Kis was appreciative of his train of thought and reasoning. That he picked up a grain or two of Jeremy's enthusiasm. That he probably remembered a few details of his upbringing. That, maybe, a window of engagement was becoming ajar. But Jeremy hadn't pushed it.

It had been Kis' turn to speak: 'You have done projects like this for I don't know how many years. You have invested personal capital in your ideas and often with spectacular results. I admire you for that. And then you became a rich trader. Now it looks as if you have gone back to your old beat. Why?'

'I will tell you later', Jeremy had replied, 'meanwhile I have to ask you a favour. Next week we have a Steering Committee meeting. You know most of the people present, or, at least they know you. I would like you to be there.' 'Done deal', Kis had replied. They had finished their whiskeys and had gone to bed.

Thirty-three

The clouds over the crater had not lifted. In fact, when the guide awoke Jeremy and Kis just before midnight it had started to rain. Not the downpour that is customary in April or November but yet a steady drizzle. The guide put it bluntly in front of them: 'You want to go for it?' Kis looked at Jeremy and Jeremy looked at Kis and almost in unison the two men said: 'Of course!'

The final ascent had been planned in such a way that the Uhuru Peak would be reached just before sunrise. It would be a hike of six hours and the weather might take a turn for the better. They took off and the porters used their flashlights to guide the small group on the trail. There was a notion of eeriness around this caravan. No moon, no stars, black darkness and a sparse supply of oxygen. The group treaded carefully.

The weather did not take a turn for the better: the wind picked up, the temperature dropped sharply and the rain changed into a full-blown snow blizzard. They were now in the clouds and the visibility was reduced to next to nothing. The combination of wind, cold, darkness and lack of oxygen started to take its toll on Jeremy and Kis. They were fit and sporty, but these were rather challenging circumstances: they struggled. The guide noticed and asked: 'You want to continue?' The friends said 'Yes', but it sounded less convincing than a few hours ago. The wind got stronger and now howled and growled as if to say: 'Stay of my mountain!'

Jeremy noticed that his senses dulled; he was less aware of his environment and began to hallucinate: what have I done with my life? What should I have done? What should I *do*? What am I doing on this mountain? What is a mountain? Sarah calls me: my "mountain". Where is Sarah? Why isn't she here?

And then he fell. No, he slipped on the trail and then he fell off the trail. He rolled, he bounced, he yelled and then there was silence.

The guide immediately got into action mode: 'Jeremy, are you OK?' he shouted and jumped into the void where Jeremy had disappeared.

Thirty-four

After Anthony's visit, Sarah had randomly consulted her real estate portfolios. Not really hers, but those of her contacts, who knew that Sarah had good connections and wanted her to be informed of choice properties on the market. Anthony had left an impression on her and she had felt an inclination to work with him, to make him happy. Sarah had consciously reflected on her sessions with Henri and had decided to review her client list and to weed out, well, yes, what she now considered "weeds". But Anthony, although a newcomer, did not fall into that category. She brought his features – tall, handsome, muscular and, of course African – back from her memory and tried to visualize him in a physical environment. Yes, she could see him in between walls and also perceive colour schemes around him – ochre, green, yellow – and furniture pieces: lots of ebony. While playing the mind game – which she enjoyed doing – Sarah also saw a horizontal piano in Anthony's virtual interior. Strange, she thought; that had not been an original idea before. Yes, there had been customers who had insisted on putting a piano in one of their rooms, but more as an afterthought than as a starting point. Why would she see Antony's interior rather differently and have that piano there from the outset, not even knowing whether he played the piano?

When Sarah asked herself that question she realized that there was no way of checking his ideas with him. He had given her a card with a name and that was it! No telephone number, no other contact details, nothing. Yet, she was putting more creative energy in this enigmatic Anthony Leiser than in many of her confirmed clients. Was there a reason?

Something began to dawn on her; it was Henri's message: "Let your heart lead the way!" Whether Anthony would contact her again, or not, finding and decoration an apartment for him, in the virtual sense, gave her a lot of pleasure. And then, she felt, she would see this man again and be ready for his return.

There was another thought, rather more scary, that entered her mind: was she doing this because of Anthony's Arusha connection? Was she still expecting Jeremy to return?

Thirty-five

Jeremy had broken a leg. The guide had expertly addressed the situation, a tent had been pitched, an emergency splint been constructed and administered, and a porter been dispatched to mobilize a rescue team. Jeremy had been carried off the mountain on a stretcher, an ambulance had taken him to the Kilimanjaro Christian Medical College, an X-ray photo had shown a clean fracture, plaster had been applied and now Jeremy was walking around with the help of crutches. Car driving was out of the question and so was cycling.

Jeremy and Kis were having a drink in the beer garden, next to Jeremy's office, three days after the accident when Jeremy finally began to wake up to reality. 'Kis, I could have been dead. Wasn't it for that small ridge that broke my fall, I would have been history.'

'I don't believe in coincidence. Obviously, there is a reason for me to have survived. I don't know what it is, but I think there is a signal and I will heed it. For starters, I have an admission to make: I have not told you the full truth when I suggested that you would come over to climb Kili with me. The truth is that I want you to run the flower project.'

Jeremy had his broken leg on a stool in front of Kis, and looked Kis in the eyes. There was a deafening silence between the two guys, but a silence loaded with electrifying thoughts. Had Kis been tricked by Jeremy? Had Jeremy paid the price for that with his broken leg? Jeremy and Kis continued to look at each other, each immersed in their own thoughts. Finally Kis broke the silence. He got up and hugged Jeremy. 'You big son of a bitch!' he said.

Thirty-six

It had been two months since Sarah had started seeing Henri and she had gradually changed her routines. She had reduced her client portfolio and allocated more time to her design work. It was financially less rewarding than selling all-in packages to wealthy clients, but there was a spiritual pay-off: a greater connect with the "self". Sarah was aware that she still had a stretch to go and that she would need the likes of Henri Lemaire to accompany her on her voyage. She did not know her destiny, but for the moment she seemed to enjoy the road towards it.

She had also decided to take out more time for herself. No, she would not go on a long adventurous vacation this year. She admitted a newly felt fear of solitude. For the time being she would need her work, her office, and her house and hearth as some form of protection for her fragile condition. And, last but not least: Terry.

They had become really good friends and often spent chunks of time together outside the office – galleries, shows, luncheons – and Sarah would not want to let go of her presence. They talked a lot, laughed a lot and could be seen as two young women who happily coasted through life. But both of them were aware that there were limits to their openness.

Terry remained conscious of the fact that she was an employee and Sarah seemed to feel a certain discomfort, guilt even, about her "crisis". She didn't want to revisit that episode and neither did Terry. Nevertheless, Sarah considered Terry a form of protection; she would not want to leave her behind.

It was a beautiful summer day and Sarah had spent a productive morning in her atelier. She had been working on curtains and, inadvertently, she had felt inspired by Anthony, or, at least, what she *thought* was Anthony. Her designs were panels of brown and red, brought together by playful yellow braids. Sarah had been pleased with the result, very pleased.

Having put her colour pencils down, she shouted to Terry: 'Let's go for lunch. I pay!' 'Where do you want to go?' Terry responded from her desk. 'Shall I make a reservation?' '"Café du Théatre"', Sarah suggested. 'Terrace, please.'

When they arrived at the Café, Fernando was standing in the doorway. 'Well, well', he said with a straight face. 'The dead have arisen from their graves. That's to say, some of them. What about Mr de Besançon? I haven't seen my preferred customer for ages. Not even received a postcard!' Sarah froze and Fernando noticed. He quickly took another tack: 'Ladies, you make more than up for Jeremy's absence. Please follow me to your table.'

They sat down and before Fernando had handed them the menu Sarah had already ordered a bottle of Chardonnay. Since Jeremy, she had continued drinking a glass of wine occasionally and enjoyed that with Terry, but in moderation, not a bottle at the time.

'Are we celebrating something?' Terry asked when the wine was served. 'I propose a toast to our friendship', Sarah said. 'To us', Terry replied, but sensed that there was something else on Sarah's mind. They ordered their favourite food (same choice for both of them: half a dozen of oysters – marennes Oléron –, followed by grilled sole) and began to talk. Nothing serious: light stuff.

And then Sarah began to cry. Not like in the old days; this was a light drizzle compared with the downpours of two months ago, Terry thought and gently touched Sarah's hand. 'What's wrong?' Sarah took a Kleenex out of her bag and dried her eyes. 'I don't' know, Terry. I'm trying very hard to follow the path that Dr Lemaire has shown me. I discover new aspects of life and make an effort to adjust, to get closer to the "self". You know that I've changed my habits and work routine and that I attempt to steer away from the "control" sphere, that I spend more time on the creative part of my work, but – and her it comes – I cannot get Jeremy out of my system. There is a strange thing happening. Once I told you that I felt like a puppet with strings being pulled by an unknown player.

That feeling is still there. You remember this gentleman from London, Mr Leiser? I feel his presence and in my head I have designed the interior of his apartment, which he hasn't even selected! When I was doing work on curtains this morning I felt inspired by him. Strange, isn't it? Mr Leiser was born in Arusha, where Jeremy started his new life. Somehow I feel that there is a link between the two men. And then, when we entered the restaurant, Fernando mentioned Jeremy's name. It's all a bit overwhelming and to tell you the truth: in spite of all my efforts to forget Jeremy, I miss him terribly!' Sarah started to cry again.

Fernando arrived to serve the oysters and professionally ignored the emotions palpably present around the table. 'Ladies, please enjoy your Olérons', he wished and disappeared.

Terry felt like reacting to Sarah's confession before enjoying her meal. 'Sarah, thank you for sharing your emotions with me', she said. 'I believe it is wonderful to be sensitive to circumstances as you just described: your emotions when designing curtains or virtual interiors. Where Jeremy features in all of that I don't know. And then this Mr Leiser: I had him on the phone for 30 seconds, so I don't know him. If you think that he could play some part in your "puppet-on-a-string" discomfort I would be happy to help you trace him. But my hunch is that it might be useful to check out with Dr Lemaire once more. You haven't seen him for some time. Anything wrong with giving him a call?'

'OK, I will', Sarah responded, 'and can we now change the subject and enjoy our lunch? Cheers!'

Fernando appeared. 'Ms Appleton?' 'Yes, Fernando', Sarah replied, and thought: how does he know my name? She had been at the Café for business engagements, but without revealing her name. With Jeremy she had been simply Jeremy's companion. 'Excuse me, but Mr Leiser asked me to give this to you', Fernando said, handed her a card and left.

204

Thirty-seven

'Listen', Jeremy said after he had ordered another round of drinks, 'regrettably we did not reach the Peak, hopefully some other time. My accident was not planned, but it has changed one or two things. I am a bit handicapped right now and will have to adjust my schedule. I have some ideas as to how go about that, but obviously there might be some inconvenient delays in the execution of the project. I am not suggesting that you decide here and now how to become involved in the long term. What I'm asking you is to consider helping with the short term issues.'

'I think that I can do that', Kis replied, 'but now that you've admitted that you've tricked me into this business I believe that I'm entitled to some revenge in the form of a wish. But first I have a proposal to make and that is this: you give me full insight into your plans, – short and long term. We will together study all details and agree on them. You have announced my presence at the next meeting of the Steering Committee, which will be in two days. We will have to speak with one voice and to defend one point of view. Of course, the members of the Steering Committee are entitled to their opinions and we will listen to those. We will ask for decisions to be made. Afterwards I will return to London and reflect on my future involvement in the project.'

'Slightly changing the subject: may I ask you something? Did your fall have anything to do with Sarah and, if so, don't you think that the time has come to recognize that?'

Jeremy was quiet for some time. He did remember the moments of confusion before he slipped and also that Sarah had been in his mind at the time, but what was the significance of that? 'Maybe', he replied, 'but what should I "recognize"?'

Kis took another sip of his drink and looked Jeremy in his eyes. 'I think I know your story and I respect you for leaving Sarah the way you did. In fact, I believe that you have been very courageous. Meanwhile, two months have passed, two months during which you have buried yourself with work, maybe in an attempt to forget Sarah. Was your subconscious asking for some kind of recognition, on Kili, and caused your fall? Should you not do something with that signal – as you have called it yourself – other than admitting that you tricked me?'

Kis laughed and Jeremy joined in. The two men felt relieved; there had been a lot of stress over the last few days, physical and psychological. Now that all was said and done there was a sense of liberation, and of excitement about what life still had in store

'I get your point, Kis, and thank you for bringing it up', Jeremy said. 'Yes, it is true that since my arrival I've been working like an idiot. Maybe I was trying to suppress something or to make a point. Off late my mother often enters my mind. You know how fond I am of her and how much I enjoyed our times together. How much she has given me. Am I trying to give something back? Am I looking for some kind of substitute? In the form of my work? In the shape of Sarah? I think the question I'm asking me is: am I doing things for the right reasons?'

'I wouldn't know', Kis reacted, 'but asking yourself questions is useful and answers will eventually come. The fact that we're having this discussion I consider very meaningful and I would like to take it a little further. You probably remember the Swahili expression: "Kupoteya njia ndiyo kujua njia".' 'Yes, I do', Jeremy replied. 'It means: "To get lost is the way to learn".'

'Correct', Jeremy responded. 'It's an old proverb, but still very true. Now my wish: I would like you to create time and space for reflections, I wish that you don't consider this flower project the end of the world, that you won't be afraid of failure – which, by the way, is in the same equation as success – and that you're aware, as your accident shows, that you're not indestructible.'

Kis went on: 'You told Sarah that she was probably at some crossroads in her life. You might be in a similar position. I am not a psychoanalyst, but I know you as a friend. You're a very strong-willed individual and that has served you in your undertakings. You have become very successful, but once more: you're not indestructible.'

The two men were silent for a moment and then it was Jeremy's turn to speak: 'Kis, I think you're right and I'm grateful to you for putting your thoughts in such an honest way to me. You're a real friend. I will heed your advice and carefully revisit my motives, actions and perceived values. Your wish has been granted. But tell me: do you think I acted wisely with Sarah?'

'I believe that I already told you that I admire you for your courage', Kis replied. 'But I'm not a judge of your actions. Time will tell. Nevertheless, my gut feeling tells me that you did the right thing. And now something else: you have admitted that you tricked me. I also have an admission to make. I left a message for Sarah with Fernando. The message reads "Kupoteya njia ndiyo kujua njia".'

'WHAT?' Jeremy exclaimed, 'you did *that?* When? And why didn't you tell me?'

Kis calmly responded: 'When you called me and asked to contact Sarah I acted according to your instructions. But, being your friend, I felt entitled to participate in your scheme of things. My meeting with Sarah made an impression on me. When I left the Café Sarah stayed behind. I scribbled a message on the back of the Anthony Leiser card, left it with Fernando and asked him to give it to Sarah if and when she would return. It was done on impulse, as if I wanted to toy with fate. I know Sarah is your business, but I have no regrets having gotten a bit involved in the act. So there you have it. Both Sarah and you got the same message. And after what you've done to me: you and I are even!'

Jeremy, with the help of his walking stick, got up and moved towards Kis. He threw his free arm around him and said: 'Kis, I love you. You're a wonderful friend, but a cunning one!'

Thirty-eight

Sarah looked at the card. Anthony Leiser it said, in a fine classical print, nothing else. Why would Fernando give her a business card she had already received from the person himself? She turned the card over and noticed a handwritten text: "Kupoteya njia ndiyo kujua njia". What could be the meaning of that? She showed it to Terry.

'No idea', Terry said, 'but after what you told me just a few minutes ago, I guess we are talking serious sign language here. You said that Mr Leiser was born in Tanzania and my hunch is that the message is written in his mother tongue. Having it translated is not too difficult and I can help you with that. Interpreting it is another story, but let's not jump the gun. My immediate question is: why did he leave this card with Fernando? He could have communicated with you directly and how did this Mr Leiser know that we would have lunch here today? Shall we ask Fernando?'

Sarah reacted right away and beckoned Fernando to the table. 'Do you know anything more about this?' she asked and held the card in front of Fernando's face.

'Ms Appleton', Fernando replied with offended dignity, 'Mr Leiser left this card with me after your get-together some weeks ago. He asked me to give it to you at the earliest occasion. I'm only the messenger, please don't shoot me! Would the ladies care for anything else to drink?' 'Yes, please', Sarah replied, 'another glass of Chardonnay!'

And then she turned to Terry: 'What a day! You're right; another session with Dr Lemaire might be called for.'

Thirty-nine

Jeremy and Kis went to work. Jeremy's plans were spread out on his office table. All his calculations were meticulously reviewed, his assumptions questioned and his projections challenged. Kis threw in a number of observations with respect to the production side of things – 'don't forget there are different and often opposing clans in the Chagga tribe' – and had quite a few suggestions where it came to marketing, like creating name brands and ensuring customer loyalty.

'That's why I want you to be part of the show', Jeremy had simply reacted, but he realized with a bit of a shock that his mind had no longer the same focus of purpose as when he had arrived in Arusha. Was it his accident or Kis' remarks afterwards that gave him this floating feeling? Yes, he wanted this flower project to succeed and he knew that he was capable of pulling it off. Kis seemed to be ready to play his part and that was a formidable security. Why this aloofness? Would it be that the "what's next" question started to rear its head? Was it Kis' message: "to get lost is to learn the way" that had not been fully understood? 'I am not lost', Jeremy said to himself and then decided to put his thoughts to rest. In two days' time they would have the Steering Committee meeting and that would be a crucial one. This was not the moment to ponder the imponderables.

Forty

Kis was warmly welcomed at the meeting and greeted with "where-have-you-been-all-this-time?" Of course, there were quite a few questions about Jeremy's plastered leg. 'Is this what your friend does to you when he comes to visit?' someone asked. The atmosphere was relaxed and Jeremy felt comfortable when he called the meeting to order.

'Ladies and gentlemen, before we come to business I would like to make a few personal remarks. First of all, as I announced last time we met, I'm happy to formally welcome Kis. Most of you know him as a respected son of this country and this region. Kis is also my best friend and I feel honoured that he has agreed to help us in our joint endeavours. It is my wish that today we can explore ideas as to the form and shape of his future contribution. Secondly, you've noticed that I'm slightly handicapped. Kis and I decided to climb Kili and I fell. Fortunately I am here to tell the story, but, honestly, I could have been dead.'

'I'm not shy to tell you that my accident has taught me a lesson. A lesson for me, but also a lesson for what we collectively are trying to accomplish. We should not rely on any singular individual or singular component for our project to become a success. It is true that I have made a commitment

215

towards the project and I will stick to it. But I cannot be regarded as the single, omnipotent force for it to succeed. Again, my promises with respect to guiding its progress, to guaranteeing loan capital, to providing working capital and other forms of engagement, stand. However, the events on Kili have made me think; in fact, it is my friend Kis who helped me articulate those thoughts.'

'My conclusion is this: Kis and I have reviewed, very carefully, all plans and the results of tests done so far. We would like to present them to you and to invite you to agree on the way forward. I sincerely hope that we can count on Kis to help us along. But I will have to take a step back. For my own benefit and, more importantly, for that of the project.'

There was cutthroat silence in the meeting room. The Steering Committee members looked around for someone to break it. Chairs were moved, throats were cleared, but no word was uttered. It was Kis who finally broke the ice.

'My brothers and sisters', he said in Swahili and then continued in English: 'Jeremy has made an important statement just now. I was with him on Kili and afterwards. I know this man well. I know his honourable intentions and his courage. I'm proud to be his friend.

'Jeremy, at the request of Mzee, started this project. Over the last few days we've looked together over all the technical and commercial details. We believe that we are onto something that is potentially very rewarding, but the outcome depends on all of us. Not on Jeremy and me alone. Jeremy has just announced that he would like to take a step back. Obviously, his broken leg will limit his mobility in the short term, but that's not the issue. After his accident on Kili he may now look at life somewhat differently.'

It was still very quiet in the meeting room; the Committee members were at a loss as to where Kis was heading. Kis looked around the table, fixing his eyes on the members one by one. Finally he said: 'But I make you a promise, here and now. It will be either Jeremy or me, but we will not let you down!'

The members of the Steering Committee stood up and collectively burst into a chant: 'Bravo, bravo!' Jeremy, sitting next to Kis, gave him a big hug and said: 'Wow, what an acceptance speech!' Kis leaned over and whispered in Jeremy's ear, for nobody to hear: 'Not so quickly, my friend. We've got still quite a stretch to go.'

Forty-one

Terry had figured it out, the Swahili proverb, and she had told Sarah, and Sarah had made an appointment with Lemaire. Meanwhile all sorts of thoughts had gone through her head. Who was this Anthony Leiser? Why had he wanted her to have this message? Sarah had no problem with its content, but why would a stranger approach her with a rather personal thought? And why would this be delivered on the very same day that she had felt inspired by him in the design of new curtain panels? Sarah was more and more inclined to believe that there was a Jeremy connection, but what could it be? She was doing her level best to find herself and to forget Jeremy, but it looked as if there were powerful forces at work to prevent her from doing so. "To get lost is the way to learn", the Swahili expression said. Should she travel to Arusha to find out its true meaning?

'Henri', Sarah began, after she had set down in his office, 'I've had some strange experiences since we last met and I would like you to help me in finding their meaning.'

'Sarah, we're here to help', Henri responded and gave her one of those warm smiles she had grown attached to. 'But before you give me the "strange things" story, could you please provide me with an update on where you've reached on the, maybe not so strange, subjects we've been discussing?' 'OK, fine', Sarah reacted, being uncomfortably aware of the 'control issue' that had been part of those.

In a random fashion Sarah gave Henri an account of the recent changes in her life. How she had tried to be conscious of her thoughts and actions, how she had made an effort to make decisions with her heart rather than with her head, how she had changed her work habits, both in form and content, how she had revisited her childhood and had readjusted her interpretation of the roles of both her father and her mother in her upbringing: her father was no longer the absolute hero, her mother no longer the despicable villain. That she would try to reconnect with her twin brother. And she went on and on, zigzagging through emotional and psychological fact and assumption.

Sarah paused. 'And I've also decided to stay put this year and not to go on a long adventure journey, to continue working on myself', she said, as if to announce that she had arrived at the end of her story. 'Sounds good to me', Henri reacted. 'What about those "strange things"?'

'I don't seem to get Jeremy out of my head. I'm constantly reminded of his brief existence in my life and whenever that happens I'm being thrown off course; it feels as if all the progress I'm making is annulled with one sharp blow. As if I have to start over again.'

'And then there is this, what I could almost call Voodoo sensation.' Sarah proceeded to introduce Mr Leiser and gave a full account of his visit, the way he inspired her design work off late and the message on his card, delivered by Fernando a few days ago. 'And I think there is a link between Mr Leiser and Jeremy', she said by way of concluding her statement.

Henri reacted rather seriously: 'Quite a character, this Mr Leiser. I don't know where to place him, but I agree with his Swahili expression. In a way you were lost when you decided to come and visit me. That is not necessarily a negative "condition" and that is what the Swahili proverb hints at: an opening, a new beginning. Maybe your "strange things" story becomes less "strange" when we look at it in the context of what you told me earlier. You said that you're making progress in finding your "self". That's wonderful, but you know that it's not a straight line; neither can you think of recovery – if I may use the word – as an overnight phenomenon.'

'You remember our discussions some time ago when you asked me: "How long is this going to last?" I could not give you an answer. It's a roller-coaster ride on which you have just embarked. The process can ultimately be measured in time and effectiveness, but not on a daily basis and that can be rather unsettling. What you have been trying to do since we met first was to question some certainties you thought you *had* in your life, but that does not automatically imply that new ones immediately present themselves. That makes you vulnerable and uncertain.'

Lemaire paused to allow Sarah to react. When she didn't, he continued: 'Now Jeremy. At the peak of your "crisis" – again a word, nothing more - Jeremy appears and right away your devil ego adopts him as your saviour. Not for nothing you called Jeremy "my mountain". That ego of yours, that little devil, does not like to give up. His survival, in part, *depends* on the Jeremy character. He uses every opportunity to make you believe that your happiness hinges on him. In all your vulnerability you have little resistance to this devil's manipulations and you, temporarily, crash. Nothing wrong with that, as long as you are aware of what's happening.'

Henri smiled at Sarah and Sarah smiled back. 'Henri, you want to come to Arusha with me to find this devil?' Sarah said in laughter. Henri burst out in laughter too: 'I know that you're joking and that's a very good sign. Jeremy is not the devil and you know that.'

'You asked me once: "How do I get Jeremy back?" My response was: "Do nothing." I believe that you've become aware that it is not Jeremy, that it is *your* struggle. You've faced that struggle head-on and you're making a lot of progress. Whether there is room for a Jeremy in your life one day I cannot say. Eventually you'll find out. The priority of the moment is to stay the course and to accept the ups and downs as part of the process. Be conscious of them and live your emotions! By the way: I wouldn't mind meeting this Leiser fellow one day.'

Sarah got up and took his hand: 'Thank you, Henri. That was very useful. You will not go to Arusha with me; neither will I go, at least not now. But I'm grateful for your company on the road travelled so far. I'll give you a call for an appointment in future.'

'Pretty much still in charge?' Henri said with a chuckle as he led her out of his office.

Forty-two

Jeremy and Kis were sitting on Mzee's terrace, enjoying their whiskey. They were relaxed, after a few hectic days in Moshi. The Steering Committee had approved their plans and a date had been set for their formal submission. Jeremy and Kis had together conducted a few more field visits and afterwards they had moved to Arusha to spend time with Mzee before Kis' return to London.

'Do you remember how long ago it is that you and I were sitting here for the first time?' Jeremy asked. 'Yes, I do', Kis replied, '20 years.' 'And do you realize how little has changed?' Jeremy continued and pointed at the Mount Meru which was showing its majestic head against the setting sun. 'Isn't it magnificent?' Kis replied in agreement. 'And do you realize how *much* has changed since you showed me the Steinweg?' 'Yes', Kis replied, 'you could say that. But knowing you, you're about to tell me something. Why don't you get it off your chest?'

Jeremy was silent for a while and took another sip of whiskey. He leaned back and closed his eyes. Yes, the Steinweg changed my life, he thought. Hadn't it been for that encounter with that particular instrument I would have returned to London and probably would have become a rich

225

banker with a boring office and an equally boring family life. Instead, I stayed in Africa and discovered different human values and the rewards of giving.

'Kis, you know my story. I don't have to go back to it. Why did I say what I just said? Because I think I'm going through another life-changing moment. I'm talking about it because you're my friend and I would like to give the forces of life the space to run their show. Talking to a friend, for me, creates that space. You and I have talked after the Kili accident. I'm grateful for the views you expressed. I told you that I would take time out for reflection. I've done that and will continue doing so.'

The two friends stayed on the veranda hours after the sun had set. A good part of the contents of the whiskey bottle accompanied them in their discussions. Mzee left them in peace; he knew that the two men had something important between them and that they should not be disturbed. He had asked the cook to wait with serving dinner. Mzee was very happy with the presence of Jeremy and Kis under his roof and was sorry to see Kis leave tomorrow.

What had precisely transpired between the two friends in Moshi Mzee would have no way of knowing; he had not asked questions. He remembered his discussions with Jeremy, when Jeremy had told him about his plans to return to Europe and to let Kis take his place in Moshi. He had promised confidentiality and he would not break his promise. Mzee also had not probed into the circumstances of Jeremy's accident, although he had the feeling that this young man had changed somewhat since then. He had found Jeremy a bit more contemplative, introspective, less expressive. It had not bothered Mzee; he had seen a lot of things in his life and he had learned to succumb to the forces of life. Yet, didn't he still have a role to play?

Finally the two men entered the house. 'Sorry, to keep you waiting, father', said Kis. 'No problem, son', Mzee replied. 'I guess, you guys had something important to discuss', and he took his place at the head of the dining table. Dinner consisted of duckling cooked with coconut milk, a traditional dish served for an honoured guest. They ate in silence; then Mzee cleared his throat. He wanted to speak, Jeremy knew, and sensed that there would be an important message.

'My sons', Mzee started, 'I'm grateful for the days we've spent together. I'm also grateful for the work the two of you are doing, for what you're trying to accomplish. Not for yourselves, but for the people of Moshi. I know you both and I'm sure you will succeed.'

'When I was a young man I was like the two of you, energetic, ambitious and resourceful. I was formed like that by my

227

father. My father was an honest man, driven by compassion for his fellow human beings. He gave a lot and was rewarded plentiful. Still today I am grateful for what he taught me. I've tried to follow his example and if one considers me successful businessman I owe that to him.'

'I also have tried to set an example for Kis, my only son. He also has become a successful businessman and accumulated great wealth. I'm sure he is using this wealth for a good purpose. What I hope is that he doesn't forget his roots: he is an African. Kis has decided to live in Europe, but his values originate in the plains of Kilimanjaro. The values of his ancestors, of his grandfather, of his father.'

'I'm an old man now and have not many more years to live, but I still have one wish. This flower project, I would like to see succeed. I would like it to be the "thank you" to all that life has given to me. After that, the gods may take me away from this earth.' Mzee stopped and proceeded finishing his plate.

You cunning old bastard, Jeremy thought affectionately. Typical Mzee: not beating about the bush, but delivering his messages in measured doses. Now let's see how Kis reacts.

Kis reacted: 'Father, you know that words can only say so much. You *know* that I'm grateful for all that you have given me. You *know* that I am who I am thanks to you. You *know* that I consider my wealth not my property. You *know* that I will never forget my African roots. What are you trying to tell me?'

Mzee looked Kis in his eyes and simply said: 'Come back.'

Forty-three

'Sarah, I've got Mr Leiser on the phone for you', Terry shouted from behind her desk. Sarah's heartbeat went on the double. She took a deep breath and replied: 'I'll take it.'

'Sarah Appleton', she confided to the receiver, as cool as she could manage. 'Hello, Sarah, this is Anthony Leiser. I hope you remember me.' How could I not, Sarah thought. 'Unexpectedly, I'm in town and I wonder whether you would have time for a chat. I'm sorry for not having given you advance notice, but you know how it is in business. I happen to be here now and tonight I'm flying out to London. Would lunch be all right for you?'

Sarah looked at her watch: it was eleven o'clock. Yes, she would be free for lunch and she would love to see this mystery man, but what was good advice here? Should she play hard to get?

Sarah couldn't think clearly and rather meekly said: 'Yes, I remember you, Anthony. Let me see. Yes, I think I could make time for you today. You said lunch?' 'That would be a great pleasure', Anthony replied. 'Twelve o'clock at the "Café du Théatre"?' 'All right', Sarah said without thinking and hung up.

Sarah rested her head in her hands, dizzy: what had she just done? Had she again allowed Jeremy to gatecrash into her life and interfere with her recovery process? Was she letting the Jeremy-Anthony-Café du Théatre connection abuse her vulnerability? Or was she just making it all up?

Sarah went to Terry's desk and set down in front of her. 'Mr Leiser proposed lunch and I said "yes", but I feel terribly uncomfortably with it all. Do you have any idea as to what might be going on?'

Terry looked at Sarah and saw a troubled face; the same strains of despair, that had been so visible a few months ago, but which had since largely disappeared.

'No, I don't know what's going on. When are you going to learn to let life run its course?' Terry was shocked hearing herself speak like that. That was harsh language, language one should certainly not use when speaking to a boss. Sarah quickly took her embarrassment away: 'Thank you, Terry. I guess that's just what I needed to hear!'

Forty-four

'You're welcome, Ms Appleton.' Fernando stood in the doorway and extended his hand. 'Please, let me guide you to your table.' What's this? Sarah thought, how come he's expecting me? She was even more surprised when Fernando brought her to "Jeremy's table", where Anthony was reading his newspaper.

Anthony got up as soon as he saw her. He smiled warmly, shook her hand and said: 'Sarah, so good to see you and so nice of you to have accepted my invitation. Please sit down and what would you like to drink?' Fernando was waiting at a discreet distance. Sarah hesitated; she was tempted to say: something *very* strong, but she said nothing. Anthony decided for her: 'Fernando, please bring us a bottle of 98 Ermitage de Chasse Spleen.'

Sarah set down; she *had* to: her knees wobbled. The Chasse Spleen was the wine Jeremy had ordered the first time they had dinner here, at this very same table. This was too much to be called coincidence! She had on several occasions felt like a puppet on a string; right now she felt like a fly caught in a spider's web. She took a deep breath and for the first time since she had entered the Café she opened her mouth:

'Anthony, good to see you too.' That was all she managed to say.

She looked at Anthony. He smiled at her and Sarah wished to die there and then. 'Excuse me for a moment, please', she said and left for the ladies' room. She put her face under the cold water tap, dried her face, repeated the exercise, took a few deep breaths, looked in the mirror and told that other person: 'It's all right, whatever it is.'

When she came back to the table the wine had been served. They clinked glasses and then Sarah said: 'Now, Anthony, where were we?'

Anthony smiled again: 'You tell me. Any ideas since we last met?' Sarah did not reply right away. She certainly did not want to tell Anthony that, in her head, she had already created his apartment and that Anthony had been a source of inspiration in her other design work. She simply said: 'If and when you're ready I think we can work together. I've looked at a number of properties that might interest you and, if you so wish, I can help you in decorating the apartment of your choice.'

I'm not doing well, Sarah thought. This is not the way to hook a potential client. Have I lost my touch? Anthony didn't give her much time to find an answer to her question. 'That's wonderful!' he said. 'Can you give me some detail?' Sarah tried, but she couldn't. In front of this man she was speechless and her mental functions were blocked.

Sarah took a sip of her wine and another one. 'How was your business trip?' was all she could come up with. 'Rather exciting', Anthony replied. 'A combination of business and pleasure. All in all, quite successful. And, by the way, the last time we met you asked me about a certain Kis. I was introduced to him while transiting in Nairobi. We had a brief chat. I asked him about this friend of yours. Could his name be Jeremy? He mentioned that name and told me that he had seen him recently. I believe it was in Arusha.'

Sarah's heart stopped beating. 'Anything else?' was the only thing she managed to utter. 'Yes, I believe that he had an accident', Anthony added matter-of-factly. Sarah took another sip of her wine, almost choked in it and started to cry.

Anthony took her hand, but didn't say anything. He just let her cry. When Sarah regained her composure she started a long monologue, giving Anthony the whole package, in bursts of words, from the day she met Jeremy until her last visit with Lemaire. 'Wow, quite a story', Anthony reacted, when he sensed that all was said. 'You certainly have gone through a lot. But, may I ask, why are you telling me all this?'

Sarah thought: I've gone this far, I could as well go all the way, and said: 'Because I think that somehow there is a link between you and Jeremy.' Anthony looked at her. 'I see', was all he said. 'And why did you leave me this card?' Sarah added, almost angrily.

Forty-five

Jeremy had hired a driver to take him back to Moshi and to ferry him around on his business. Fortunately, most of the fieldwork had been done and now the time had come to attack the paperwork. Jeremy spent a good portion of each day behind his desk, making calculations, drafting project documents, loan agreements and other legal stuff. It was not his favourite occupation, but it needed to be done and the day of the formal submission of it all was approaching rapidly. Fortunately Tira was there to help him in putting it all in an attractive package. She had held a position with the National Development Corporation and knew the required formats by heart. She also looked after Jeremy's personal life: brought him food and refreshments and saw to it that his house was kept in order.

Because of his plastered leg Jeremy didn't go out as often as he used to and often spent his evenings at home. He sensed that he had become calmer since his accident and enjoyed being by himself, letting thoughts come and go. He was learning to step out of his body, or out of his mind rather, and to become an observer of what was happening to him: watching streams of thought as if they were ticker messages on a display screen.

He had heeded the advice of Kis, his good friend, to reflect on his motivations and actions, and to be receptive to life's messages, even if they did not come with instruction manuals.

Kis and he had talked at length, the night before Kis' departure, on Mzee's veranda. They had discussed the flower project, but mostly they had talked about "life". It had appeared that both of them, in their own ways, were going through some soul searching episode and comparing "notes" had been very rewarding. And they had talked about Sarah or rather about Jeremy and Sarah. Jeremy had requested Kis to pay her a visit once more, which Kis had happily agreed to do. 'Give me a call afterwards', Jeremy had requested. 'I will', Kis had promised.

It was now three weeks since Kis had left and he had not called. Jeremy was not worried: he knew his friend. Kis would call when the time was right and together with the Steering Committee they had set the date for the formal presentation of the project. That would be in eight days. Kis would call, Jeremy knew.

Forty-six

'And why did you leave me this card?' Sarah asked.

Now it was Anthony's turn. 'Sarah, if you allow me to say it: I very much admire you as a person. I see great human values in you, but let me stop there. I don't have the right to pry into, or comment on, your private domain. When we talked last, you gave me a glimpse of your past; you talked about your father and your upbringing. You also told me about wanting to make changes in your life and work. You gave me the impression that you were searching, but not knowing for what and where. I was flattered with the confidence you bestowed upon me, but, again, I felt that I had no right to provide unsolicited advice. Nevertheless I wanted to encourage you on your path of discovery. On impulse, when leaving the restaurant, I scribbled something on my business card, in my mother tongue, and gave it to Fernando. "For when she comes back", I added. I'm glad you offered Fernando the opportunity to pass it on to you. If I offended you in anyway: please accept my apologies!'

'No, not at all', Sarah replied, almost in defence. 'I was just surprised.' All of a sudden she felt a certain calm come over her, not unlike what she had experienced with Jeremy, the first time they had met for dinner at "Chez Enzo". 'And thank you for your kind words', she continued.

'Tell me about this accident.' 'I believe that it was a climbing accident', Anthony responded, 'and that Jeremy broke a leg. Nothing really serious. That's all I can say. Now, if you allow me: could we please order lunch? I will have to catch a plane and before doing so I would like to discuss something else.'

'As you wish', Sarah said, still having that sense of calm, in spite of (or thanks to? – Sarah didn't know) that mysterious reappearance of Jeremy.

'What I would like to tell you', Anthony began after Fernando had taken the order, 'is that during my last trip I have decided to make some changes in my business plans. I will not open an office here, but I like this city and I wouldn't mind having a pied-à-terre. It will be a smaller proposition than what I had in mind previously, but I still very much would like you to help me.'

'With great pleasure', Sarah responded and she meant it. In fact, after her mind games of late, she could offer him the complete package here and now, but she didn't do it. Instead she said: 'I will do some homework and contact you. Can you please give me an e-mail address or phone number?'

'That would hardly be useful', Anthony replied. 'In a few days I will depart on a long voyage and may not be reachable. Meanwhile a business associate will look after my affairs. If you don't mind, I will ask him to contact you in a week or so. He knows me well and his name is Christopher Moretti'.

'But Anthony', Sarah protested, 'buying and decorating a place is a very personal thing. You cannot leave that to a business associate!'

'Wait until you meet this person and then you may decide', Anthony said, smiling brightly. 'If that's all right with you, I order coffee and then I will have to leave, I'm afraid. It was a great pleasure spending time in your company today.'

Forty-seven

Jeremy had learned a few things during his life in Africa and beyond: If you need the cooperation of the partners in your ventures you should not confront them with a fait-accompli. They should feel to be *real* partners, with a say in what concerns them and then cooperation would become a wish, not a command. Conscious of that axiom Jeremy had travelled to Dar-es-Salam to meet with the Permanent Secretary of the Ministry of Agriculture and Cooperatives, and with a Director of the National Development Corporation. He had had one-on-one meetings with the Mayor of Moshi, with the President of the Kilimanjaro Chamber of Commerce and with a range of other individuals who would be present at the make-or-break meeting which was approaching rapidly. He had listened to their observations and suggestions and he had, when possible and relevant, accommodated those in his proposals. Jeremy didn't want to take chances.

With the help of Tira, Jeremy had prepared a slide show. She had done a great job: simple messages and clear graphs. Yes, there were still refinements to be made and some arguments needed to be polished, but for that he needed Kis.

While, in his head, Jeremy saw clearly what still was to be done before the big event, and how, with the help of Kis, he would go about it, there were, at the same time, emotions that asked for recognition: at the meeting Jeremy would hand over the baton to Kis.

They had further discussed Kis' involvement in the project while having their drinks on Mzee's veranda and Kis had repeated what he had said before: that he had to go back to London and take stock before making a final decision. When Mzee had delivered his speech over dinner and had said: 'Come back', Jeremy knew: there was no option left for Kis.

But Jeremy had grown attached to the Moshi project, to the people, to the idea that he could make a difference in their lives and he would miss those sentiments. Yet, he also had his accident and his discussions with Kis and his own reflections after that. Jeremy had come to a conclusion: life wanted to take him in a different direction and he would not resist. Without telling anybody, not even Kis, Jeremy had booked a flight back to Europe.

'Hey, old man, you took your time', Jeremy said when Kis finally called. 'I have been pretty busy with the assignments you gave me, but I've made progress', Kis reacted.

'How's Sarah?' Jeremy asked impatiently. 'She sends you greetings', Kis replied in jest. 'I'll give you the story when we meet. I'll be flying out tomorrow, Saturday.'

'Great! My driver and I will pick you up. I propose we go straight to Moshi. There is still quite a bit a work to be done before our meeting on Wednesday.' 'Fine with me', Kis replied. 'See you Sunday morning' and he called off.

Forty-eight

'How did it go?' Terry asked as soon as Sarah entered the shop. 'Jeremy had an accident', she replied without hesitating. 'What?!' Terry exclaimed. 'How do you know? What happened?'

Sarah set down. She was calm and composed, Terry observed. 'Anthony met Jeremy's friend Kis, who told him. A climbing accident. Jeremy broke a leg. Nothing serious, according to Anthony.'

'What else did he say? Did you ask about this card?' It sounded as if Terry was probing, but Sarah didn't feel it that way. After all, she had confided in Terry her darkest thoughts and Terry had been of tremendous support, even this morning. Terry was entitled to the sequel and she would not hide a detail.

'Well', Sarah started, 'it was a roller-coaster. Initially I was very confused. We were seated at Jeremy's table and Anthony ordered Jeremy's favourite wine. I broke down and cried. Then something changed: I remembered the words you spoke before I left the shop: "Let life run its course", and I became calm. Yes, I asked about this card and he replied that he had sensed a certain struggle inside me when we last met and that he had wanted to leave a message of support. He sounded very honest.'

'And what about his project?' Terry wanted to know. 'To tell you the truth, we hardly talked about it. Anthony changed his mind; he will not open an office here, but is still thinking of having a pied-à-terre. He would like me to help him, but he's leaving on a long business trip. He asked me to follow-up with a business associate.'

'Is that all?' Terry insisted. 'You've been gone for two hours!' 'I know', Sarah replied with a calm voice. 'We talked about a lot of things. I even told him that I thought that there was a connection between him and Jeremy. He did not reply, other than saying: "I see". I did not insist. I enjoyed being in his company, I felt good.'

Terry looked at Sarah's face. The strains of despair, so painfully visible this morning were gone. There was a woman sitting in front of her who was in peace and harmony with life. Terry spoke: 'Sarah, you may not have landed a big fish in the commercial sense, but you've most certainly made a great leap forward in finding yourself and in accepting life as it comes!'

Forty-nine

They were sitting in Jeremy's office going over the presentations that Jeremy and Tira had produced. Yesterday, Sunday, Kis had rested a little after his night flight and then the two friends had set down to talk. 'Sarah first', Jeremy had insisted. 'I suggest that you have a stiff drink before I start', Kis had teased Jeremy.

After Jeremy had filled their glasses Kis began to tell the story about his lunch with Sarah. He gave the full picture, from Sarah's initial breakdown and her tearful account of the Jeremy episode and the Lemaire counsel, to the subsequent calmness Sarah had displayed as their luncheon progressed.

'Once more, Jeremy', Kis had said, 'I consider Sarah an extraordinary woman. What struck me, once she started to talk about you and the time the two of you spent together, is that she did not pity herself, neither had she any harsh words for your sudden departure. I had the impression that she had made some mayor discoveries: firstly, that she possessed emotions that she was not aware of, and, secondly, maybe not precisely articulated, the futility of wanting to control life. Once more, a great woman.'

'Thanks, Kis', Jeremy had reacted, 'I owe you a big favour for having taken the trouble to go and see her.'

They had looked at each other for a few moments without speaking. Then Kis had said: 'No, you don't owe me anything, on the contrary, I'm indebted to you. As promised, while in London, I reflected on the issues at hand: your invitation to become involved in the flower project, my father's request that I come back, and the consequences of all that on my current occupations and ambitions. It was not easy, but I've made up my mind. Like you, I sense that life wants to take me in a different direction and I will not resist. If the stakeholders of the flower project so wish, I will gladly assume the responsibilities of running the show. I would like to thank *you* for opening my eyes and for thinking that I can be useful to my own people.'

No more words had been spoken. The two friends had embraced each other, feeling a powerful moment of togetherness with the forces of destiny.

Fifty

'Jeremy, I have the Ministry on the line for you', Tira yelled. 'The Permanent Secretary would like to talk to you.' 'I'll take it. Thank you', Jeremy shouted back.

'I have some good news for you', the Permanent Secretary said, after he and Jeremy had exchanged greetings. 'I just had a word with the Minister. He's very excited about what you're doing and he insists on chairing our meeting.'

'Terrific', Jeremy responded, 'what wonderful news!' 'I agree', the Permanent Secretary continued, 'but he's leaving on an overseas trip today and he requests that you reschedule the meeting to next week Wednesday. Can you please do that?'

For a second Jeremy was speechless. Such a change of plans of plans could have major consequences. Then he recalled similar circumstances in his past undertakings. Contradicting the Minister is futile; don't fight him. You want to make progress? In a profane way, consider the wishes of the Minister "holy".

'Of course, Mr Permanent Secretary, we'll do the necessary and keep you informed. And, by the way, Kis arrived yesterday and brought some good news. He will tell you in person during the meeting next week. Thanks for calling.'

'What was that all about?' Kis asked. Jeremy told him. 'What I haven't told you, nor the Permanent Secretary', Jeremy added, 'is that I'm flying out next Friday. I will not change my plans, so I will not be here next week. As from this moment the project is yours.'

They burst out in laughter, the two friends, as a way to embrace the unexpected. 'All right', Kis said when they had calmed down, 'I accept, but only on two conditions: you spend every minute until your departure with me to bring me up to speed, and after your departure you will remain on stand-by for as long you and I agree.' 'Done deal', Jeremy reacted.

He looked out of the window. 'Come over here, Kis.' Kis went to stand next to Jeremy and together they watched the Uhuru Peak freeing itself from a layer of clouds, showing its majestic form in the reflecting rays of a brilliant sun. 'I don't know whether the gods have a message to convey, but at least they are smiling upon us', Jeremy said.

Fifty-one

It was a rainy, windy and chilly Monday. Sarah didn't like this kind of weather, certainly not in summer. Fortunately, over the weekend clouds had given way to the sun's generous presence. Saturday Sarah had gone out into the Ajuci Mountains for a hike. She had not gone back there since Jeremy and all of a sudden she had felt like exploring this mountain range once more. She had climbed the plateau that Jeremy had showed her and again had been in awe of its majestic surroundings. Of course, Jeremy had been in her mind, but not in a sad, melancholic way. She had felt a sense of gratefulness that he had brought her there, that he had enriched her life. While eating her sandwich in solitude she had experienced an oneness with him, even if he wasn't physically present.

Yesterday, she had gone jogging and had done so in full awareness. She had enjoyed it. 'I'm back again', she had said to the trees along the trail, but right away had corrected herself: 'I'm not *back*, I'm *here*. A different Sarah!'

But that was the weekend. Today the weather had turned foul and Sarah was out on the street. Fortunately, she didn't have to go far; the "Café du Théatre" was only a block away from her shop.

Last week Thursday, while she was visiting a client, Anthony's secretary had called: 'Mr Christopher Moretti will be in the neighbourhood coming Monday. Would it be convenient for Ms Appleton to have lunch with him?' Terry had consulted Sarah's calendar; not seeing any engagements she had agreed and blocked the time for lunch.

Now Sarah was on her way to the Café, but not looking forward to meeting this Mr Moretti. She had developed a liking for Anthony and would love working with him. It fitted in her new way of doing business: only doing things she would feel good about. This Mr Moretti was probably of the accountant type, wanting to discuss the price of things, rather than their emotional value. Anyway, the meeting had been fixed and Sarah would just have to sit it out.

Sarah arrived at the Café where she found Fernando, as prompted by a film script, at the door. 'Good day, Ms Appleton. Please hand me your umbrella and I'll take your coat.' Fernando did not wait for a reaction: he was all action. After he had taken care of the cloakroom formalities he bowed his head and said: 'Please follow me. Mr Moretti is waiting for you.' With the self-consciousness of someone who knows what he is doing and expects everyone else to be aware of that as well, he crossed the Café to a table where a gentleman, with his back to the room, was reading his paper.

Sarah froze in her steps: again it was Jeremy's table where Fernando was leading her to. She stood still, hardly able to function. She looked around for some kind of clue or escape and noticed that she was trembling like a leaf. 'No, not again', she told herself. 'I've been there, done that. I'm a new person now. I don't let myself be ruled by my devious emotions.' She took a deep breath and thought of all the lessons she had learned over the last few months. 'There is nothing happening, other than life', she almost said aloud.

Fernando was standing behind the newspaper-reading gentleman, obviously waiting to introduce Ms Appleton. Sarah took a few steps forward and noticed a walking stick hanging off the gentleman's chair. An accountant and a cripple one at that, Sarah thought, not very political-correctly. She heard Fernando say: 'Mr Moretti, your guest has arrived.' Mr Moretti did not look up; just said: 'Thank you, Fernando.' Then he folded his newspaper and turned his head, while his plastered leg remained resting on a stool.

'Hello, Sarah', the gentleman said. Nothing more.

Sarah's heart stood still. No, it did not stand still. It went in overdrive. There were a dozen Ferris wheels running through her system, with gravitas-challenging gyrations. And then everything stopped.

'Hello, Jeremy', she said. She approached him, gave him a kiss and sat down in front of him. 'Why this circus?' she simply asked. 'Don't you offer me anything to drink?'

Jeremy smiled and then Sarah got up and jumped on his lap. She put her arms around him, then took his head between her hands and kissed him, kissed him, kissed him all over his face. Jeremy let her. Fernando had put "reserved" signs on quite a few tables around theirs, but even if the place had been crowded this couple would not have behaved differently: this was their moment, their world. And an accidental audience would have enthusiastically applauded, not unlike the elements of nature did – in silence - when this couple made love on an Ajuci plateau, three months ago.

After this hurricane-force collision between two human beings Sarah adjusted her dress and took her seat. 'I guess we've got some catching up to do', she said. 'You certainly haven't come to discuss the apartment of Anthony Leiser?'

Jeremy smiled again. He had retained a picture of Sarah in his mind ever since he had left her, but today he found her x-times more beautiful, expressive and, of course, real. Jeremy replied, still smiling: 'No, I have not come to discuss Anthony's apartment, although he has given me carte blanche to do so.' Sarah touched his plastered leg. 'I heard you had an accident. Nothing serious, I hope?' 'Nothing serious and the plaster will come off tomorrow. If anything, my accident was a blessing.'

'Where shall we start?' Sarah asked. 'Let's not', Jeremy replied. 'We certainly have a lot to tell each other, but that can wait. Let's savour this wonderful moment, enjoy the present and our company to the fullest and *then* talk. Didn't you ask for something to drink?' 'All right', Sarah said, being aware of her lingering habit to wish to control things.

Jeremy waved at Fernando, who, for once, had a grin on his face, having watched the spectacle from a discreet distance. While he approached the table Sarah took out her mobile phone and dialled Terry: 'Could you please cancel my afternoon engagements? I'll explain tomorrow.'

Fifty-two

'Can we now talk? Why did you leave me?' They were laying in Jeremy's bed, Sarah resting her head in Jeremy's neck, gently drawing circles in his chest fur with her fingers. They had had their lunch but not spoken very much. The energy being exchanged between them had not needed words as a vehicle. It had been a feast of the senses, including the sixth one Jeremy had referred to on the Ajuci: the sense of consciousness, of feeling with the heart.

Afterwards they had gone to Jeremy's apartment and made love. Not the acrobatic stuff of their last encounter, three months ago; even if Jeremy's plastered leg would not have been in the way of performing circus acts: they didn't need those. It was not the sex they were after; it was the sensation of being together, of plugging their energy fields into each other's sockets.

'I did not leave you, at least not in the emotional sense.' Jeremy stroke her hair. What a wonderful woman this is, he thought, and what an exceptional gift from the universe to bring her upon my path. 'I did not leave you', he repeated. 'Yes, I did in a way.'

He paused, as if wishing to bring his thoughts together, and then he resumed: 'Our encounter, apart from the physical collision between a jogger and a cyclist, was not an accident. The intense ten days we spent together afterwards, was not a caprice of nature either. It was destiny; life wanted us to be together, but we were not ready. Both of us were in the midst of some kind of self-discovery and to consider one another the solution, the answer to our quests, would have been a terrible mistake; a short-term antidote maybe, but also a guaranteed closure on a long-term joint future.'

'I could not have said that at the time: you would not have understood, neither did I know what was happening with me. You called me your "mountain". I wanted to dismantle that image and could not think of any other way of doing that than disappearing and by doing so forcing you to face yourself. In a way, I did the same, when, ironically, I fell off my mountain. I know that I caused you a lot of pain with my brusque departure and, believe me, the last three months were not easy for me either. What kept me on my feet, save that annoying accident, were two things: my unshakeable belief in you and the knowledge that we would see each other again.'

Sarah gave him a kiss. 'You're an exceptional man, Jeremy de Besançon, but why this chicanery with Anthony?'

Jeremy closed his eyes, still stroking Sarah's hair. He did not respond and was thinking of Kis and the amazing role he had played in his eventful life.

'And?' Sarah insisted. Jeremy finally spoke up: "Well, I've told you the story about the Steinweg. How the discovery of this piano changed my life. I strongly believe that Kis and I are meant to complement each other's karmas. He is in Moshi right now, doing things I had set out to do myself. But that story is for another day.'

'Yes, I admit that I played a game with you by sending Kis to you under the Anthony cover. What I was looking for was a confirmation that you were making an effort to find yourself, so that you could make room for me, and I for you.'

'I guess that I was getting ready for another Steinweg experience, but that I wanted to have some kind of assurance that this instrument could be tuned to its full splendour. Kis helped me stay the course during those three months of solitude and, hopefully, was of some support to you as well. Fortunately, we did not do stupid things and right now we're lying in each other's arms to tell the story. May I finally say that I love you?'

'You may', Sarah said and cuddled closer to Jeremy. 'Can you please stop talking about that stupid Steinweg? My name is Sarah and I love you. Show me that you can handle *that*!'

'Still in charge?' Jeremy asked with a chuckle. 'No', Sarah reacted and gave him a kiss. 'And neither are you!'

It was pouring rain outside, but the gods were smiling right through it.

CR